THE GLORIOUS BETWEEN

THE GLORIOUS BETWEEN
A NOVEL

DOUG REID

atmosphere press

To Mary Alice Marsh

Our world is always at that instant of time when the first breath of life opens the lips and throws back the head, the instant when atoms collide and shower the universe with something new.
    Alessandra Elizabetta Marsh

PROLOGUE

THE GLORIOUS BETWEEN

Emily opened her eyes and her world became different. It was that thing in her head that was responsible; it took away her memories, and it was killing her. But Emily had blonde hair held in place with a sparkling barrette, clear green eyes, and a complexion that had not seen the sun for weeks, even months on end. She was fully formed and beautiful. She was dressed in white. Sometimes, many times, Emily felt useless and powerless, ugly and hopeless, despondent and afraid; but at other times, she felt so alive she could almost lift off the ground and walk on air. When Emily felt like that, she felt a deep joy; she felt beautiful. It was preferable to the darkness she often felt.

"Have you ever wondered why God made men and women so beautiful?" Patrick had once asked her.

"I'm not beautiful," she had responded quietly, believing she was not.

Patrick did not often smile but he did then. "Beauty is a light in the heart," he said.

She had not known how to respond and had, instead, wept. She had wept because the past is the past, forever irrecoverable.

"Kahlil Gibran," he explained softly.

"No, no, Alessandra said that," she had corrected him, remembering Alessandra looking out the window. It had been nearly spring, the garden bordering the sidewalk that led in a sweeping arc to the black paint-flaked spears opening to the greening park.

Emily opened her eyes, stood and stretched, her chin reaching her shoulder. Strands of her hair caught in the light falling around her. The soft curve of her face in profile, the light in her hair, the delicately molded shape of her forehead, nose, and mouth followed by the delicate and mysterious curve of her neck leading to her breasts. Her thin waist and her hips that reached upward as she arched her back. She released and then in a single fluid motion untied her hair, pulled it back and deftly retied it behind her head.

"Who says you are not beautiful?"

She turned to Patrick and smiled. "I am not my body," she said, leaning in and sealing what she meant with a kiss.

But in the end, we are always alone, Emily knew, and the room she suddenly found herself in, brightly lit, austere and sterile in its orderliness and hard functionality, fell into eerie quiet with only the sound of the monitoring electronics and the faint buzzing of the fluorescent lights – no sound at all – to differentiate between desolate emptiness and perfect silence. Emily gazed down at the unconscious form in the bed, the white sheet tucked up close. She adjusted the covers one last time, ensuring the body wrapped within was carefully protected, then turned and walked briskly beyond the room along a corridor of flickering lights and darkened rooms, a heart-stopping night watch with only the nearly dead. She drew her fingers over polished granite, feeling the cool hardness reach up through her and arc into her core. She was not heaven-sent and nor was she an angel; she only did what she could, but, still – and Emily felt, and not for the first time, and nor would it be the last time – that the world was far greater than what it seemed, deeper, with hidden purpose and meaning. Death, her own included, was only part of the cycle. She could understand so little, nothing really. Life in all its shades of light and dark barely made sense. But Emily could feel what Alessandra knew: we are born for no reason, we die for no reason, but everything between is glorious.

Patrick reminded her of that somehow, and that is why she loved him.

LIFE IN THE OFFING

PROMISE OF SPRING'S RETURN

With life in the offing, the promise of spring's return implicit, winter clings to the city like a shroud.

"So, tell me again about the first time we met," Emily said.

"The time I saw you, but you didn't see me, or the time after that?"

"The first-first time. How did you know it was me?"

"You were the most beautiful woman in the coffee shop."

"And...?"

"You were drinking hot chocolate."

"Ha! It must have been me then!"

Patrick laughed.

"Tell me more."

"I felt something important had happened."

"Ahh! ...Go on then! ...It was winter."

"Yes, it was; it was only a few months ago."

"Life was in the offing...."

"Yes... It was... It is. You see all the color, the music, the discord and fury, but it's all from a distance."

"Are you talking about me?" Emily asked, tipping her head.

"I am."

"Are you sure you're not talking about you?"

"No, I'm sure – I'm talking about you."

Emily laughed. "Go on, then."

With life in the offing, the promise of spring's return implicit, winter clings to the city like a shroud punctured by buildings reflecting grey sky and twisted cloud from the darkly mirrored surfaces. Rain and sleet pour down, turning to a covering sheet of ice: white and grey, snow and sand, the pure and defiled; the city is full, almost overflowing with souls with their heads down, eyes shielded, their feet in the slurry that accumulates by the curb.

"I have a soul!"

"Emily...."

"Some say I don't. I heard them talking."

"That's ridiculous."

"No, it isn't. I have no memory – nothing true. I dream my life. I am invested with God and Satan in equal measure and that's all, you see? I actually heard someone say, 'God and Satan in equal measure.' God, what an asshole! I know what I am. I am splices of film on the floor, a scratched record, photos scattered all about. Where's God in all that, I ask? Satan, maybe."

"I get it."

"There's no plot, there's just whatever pops into my head in whatever order; whatever I hear, whatever I'm told."

"Not true."

"Where's the soul in that?"

"Emily...."

"I'm just a body – a broken one at that; at least, this part up here isn't all that great." Emily tapped her head.

"Will you give me a break?"

"Keep going! I'm joking! Keep going!"

"God and Satan aside?"

"Whatever...."

For those who do not believe in the soul, the city is also inhabited by cars, buses, trucks, struggling up the icy streets, belching exhaust, their shine hidden by an encasement of salt, black snow around wheel rims and windshield wipers slapping back and forth streaking the glass, impossible to keep clean.

"I could have added paperback novels to my list of analogies – perhaps I should have."

"Emily, please...."

"You find the book – that's me, the book – just lying on the tabletop, or under the chair, front and back cover missing, whole sections torn out; you start to read but you'll never figure out what's going on."

"Is this my story or yours?" Patrick asked patiently as he sat back.

"Ha!"

"May I continue?"

"I don't know, can you? Can you begin without me telling you the 'what, where, and when'?"

"The 'what-where-when' is the coffee shop."

"Continue, then – but don't screw up."

"Screw up?"

"Don't forget any of the important parts!"

Emily laughed again, knowing she had got him on that.

THE FIRST FIRST TIME

The recent past found Patrick in a coffee shop in the lower mezzanine of McGill University Health Centre with a cup of hot chocolate, untouched, sitting before him. The shop steamed with the scent of coffee, hot croissants, and a press of cliental dressed in winter coats, scarves, and mitts. He glanced out the frosted windows to the street; it was January, the height of winter. Why let life lie dormant to await the miracle of spring; why not just let life live, Patrick wondered, still not use to the Canadian climate. Why do we inevitably need miracles to make it so? He knew why: Earth is inclined to the sun and this time of year meant winter; six months from now, summer. It is part of the inevitability and pattern of life, yet another aspect of reality we can do nothing about, only understand. It is very much like falling into a river, the current sweeping you away never to be seen or heard from again.

"A brother who is not a brother but is a brother in every way," he said to Bekele sitting across from, knowing that he would recall the reference.

Bekele slowly nodded, acknowledging their shared memory with a sad smile. It was true that Bekele was not his brother; there was no common blood mixing in their veins, but a brother he was in every other way. When Patrick turned his head, Bekele turned his; when Bekele looked up, so did Patrick.

Patrick recalled Alessandra silhouetted against the setting sun saying good night.

"Patrick and Bekele...?"

Their heads turning on their pillows.

"Thank God for each other."

Bekele – brown, athletic build, dark eyes, Ethiopian. Patrick – thin, dark hair, striking green eyes, Canadian.

Patrick imagined his home as it once had been in better days, the warmth of his bed at night, the soft pillow and the cotton sheets pulled up to his neck. The drapes lifting with the soft desert air and settling against the sill, quietly breathing in, out, and they lift again, floating in the gentle night, curled and drifting against the black of the open window and the pointed desert stars. The memory, his vision of home, existed as rhythmic music within him, the melody leading to an ache of loneliness that was with him day and night and would soar once Bekele returned home.

Patrick glanced at his brother and then looked quickly away. There were renewed tears in Bekele's eyes; how could there be tears in his eyes: this man, his brother? What was the source? Patrick knew – fire and ice, ice and fire, plucked from hell, his mortality and the mortality of all those he knew and loved, now fully revealed to him. His ship had burned to the water line off the coast.

"We like to think we hold our God-given destiny in the palms of our hands," Alessandra would say. "But sometimes the river just sweeps us along; sometimes there is nothing we can do but be brave and have faith enough to believe that it will somehow all work out."

"God, I love Alessandra!" Emily announced from her chair by the window with the frozen St Lawrence below and the snow blanketing the Laurentians to the horizon.

"You have told me that a hundred times at least; can you not think of anything else to say?"

"God, I love Alessandra!"

"That is one hundred and one."

Emily laughed. "That was funny. I'm going to put that in my journal." She lifted the small notebook up to show him. "I'm glad you told me to keep one. Here, look –." She opened the cover and turned it so he could read the content. She read it from memory. "My name is Emily Martina Portinari. I am twenty-seven years old and I can't remember a damn thing!" Emily laughed again. "That was your idea to say that, I think; I would never say anything like that!"

She suddenly pointed out the window. "Look, the river is frozen right across!"

Patrick glanced over his shoulder. It was a common sight but no less inspiring for that.

"So this is it, then, right?" Emily asked, as Patrick turned back. She continued to smile but was growing more serious too, he could see. "We are finally at the moment our individual fates intersect?" she said. "You know, fate unraveling its cloak, reaching out and drawing us together? ...You do believe in fate, don't you, Doctor Marsh?"

Patrick lifted his hands and dropped them back onto the polished surface of the desk. "Sometimes I think you are teasing me, Miss Portinari."

Emily laughed.

"Well, are you?" Patrick pressed, trying not to smile. They had explored ideas like this several times, never getting anywhere with it.

Emily imitated Patrick's seriousness to the point where he had to look away or he would smile. "We like to think we hold our God-given destiny in the palms of our hands," she said seriously and with deep gravitas, mimicking him. "But it is not true, is it? It is what we do with our fate and how we behave in the face of our fate that matters, isn't it?"

"That sounds familiar."

"It should – your mother said it. It is in here." She pointed to her journal. "On page two."

"Alessandra?"

Emily laughed. "Do you have another mother tucked away somewhere? By the way, this is my life we're sitting here discussing; this is all I have, so call me Emily." She laughed again, throwing her head back, but then suddenly leaning forward keeping her laughter in check, mimicking him again. "But please do not allow me to make impediment, Doctor Marsh! Please, do go on!" She pitched the chair forward placing her elbow on his desk, and her chin in the heel of her hand. "Please do go on."

Time folded; the sun shifted, and the moon fell in closer to the spinning Earth as Emily entered Starbucks and Patrick saw her for the first time. Blonde hair held in place with a flashing barrette that caught in the lights of the cafeteria and flashed. Beautiful and delicate, sad, hesitant, she wore a dark blue coat with a matching rose-colored scarf. She turned toward him, and he knew her instantly; he understood her completely. It was the way she turned to glance out the window to find the sun then let the rays momentarily warm her face.

He motioned to Bekele. "Do you see that woman?"

Bekele twisted about. "I agree that she looks familiar...."

"She's gorgeous; more than that. ...I think I have seen her before somewhere but I'm not sure where."

"Somewhere, maybe...."

Patrick felt a powerful sense of connection but without true memory, without history. He felt he had seen her before, but the context, the circumstances, eluded him. It was there.... He almost had it.... The memory faded, in then out. Comprehension tenuously caught on a fold. It bloomed but then faded, and then disappeared entirely. It was a mystery and he again wondered how much of the world eluded him because of the fallibility to remember accurately. The mind fails us, he knew.

"She is very nice," Bekele confirmed as he settled back. "So, when you next see our mother...," he began, beginning to smile for the first time since the accident as he realized the increasing impact the unknown woman was having on his brother. He switched, his smile opening, nodding toward her. "Why don't you go over there and say hello? What harm would there be in that, uh?"

"You are the Romeo, not me."

She sat in profile beneath the fogged window, nursing a mug of hot chocolate capped with marshmallows; she held the mug by her fingertips, gently blowing on the chocolate, waiting for the hot liquid to cool.

"I know her but I just can't place when or what the occasion might have been," Patrick repeated.

Bekele twisted around and said on his return, "She likes hot chocolate – something you have in common." He laughed quietly. "Go head, say something to her; just go over there."

Sunlight, golden like summer although it was winter, poured around her, placing her in silhouette. Heaven illuminating her, Patrick thought abstractedly. She stood, flipped her scarf about her neck, tucked her gloves beneath her arm, and buttoned her coat, then stepped toward the door which opened as if on command. She slipped through, turned, and passed by the window, dropping her chin into the folds of her scarf. Patrick was tempted to follow, but the better part of his judgment prevailed, no doubt reinforced by the presence of Bekele who never would have let him live it down if he had.

He sat back to take in the fullness and packed bustle of the shop, and noting the way the people sat in their chairs leaning in to one another, talking; seeing the way their heads turned and their eyes lifted to smile; the way the waitress slid the cups onto her tray and spun about with it lifted over her head; the way the ceiling fan gyrated, casting its shadow. The way the tracks of water slipped and entwined over the glacial surfaces of the steamed windows, he felt that all of them, every man and woman in the coffee shop that day, that hour, that minute, had become swept up into something unknowable and yet important.

"See! You recognized me right away! That means we are bound together in some way. The hot chocolate too – I think that's interesting, don't you? A common thread?"

"Not really."

"And I like the way you said I was gorgeous; I don't feel that I am, you know. I don't think I am."

"Have you looked in the mirror lately?"

Emily smiled. "You told Alessandra about me."

"So I did."

Emily thought a moment, raising her chin, keeping her smile. "Hmmm.... Keep going then."

"Well, did you get her name?" Alessandra would later ask him, told all about her by Bekele a day or two later when he was safely back in his desert home and

Alessandra in her snow-bound home, the only way out through the top floor window because there was so much snow.

"I did."

"And...?"

"I found out later, two weeks later, almost; it was quite a coincidence, really. She is an out-patient in the hospital I'm interning in." He could feel rather than see Alessandra's knowing smile through the connection that separated them.

"Ah! That's interesting! Did you get her name, or not?"

"Emily."

He imagined Alessandra's hand, long, delicate, carefully manicured fingers, flying to her heart. "Ah!"

"What's that supposed to mean, 'Ah'?" Patrick had asked, knowing exactly what Alessandra meant, but was frustrated, and embarrassed too.

"Well, Patrick...," his mother had begun, but then hesitated as if uncertain she could explain. "Don't you see?" she asked after a moment.

"I'm afraid not."

"You could not hear it in your voice – anyone who can hear would make note of it?"

"No."

"Well.... Later, then," she had said, and then quietly laughed, lightly, warmly, no doubt smiling at the mystery of what she could not, or would not, explain. "Such a lovely name!" she had whispered into the line.

"See? She and I.... You've got no idea!" Emily exclaimed.

"Emily, I..."

"Never mind! But, then again, I don't believe in fate,

do you?" Emily asked, looking up into the light, smiling an angel's smile, her hair golden in the winter light from the window.

If angels could exist, Emily would be one, Patrick thought, knowing he was being silly but knowing too he could not help himself. He was already lost. "No, I don't.... I don't know what fate has to do with any of this, but I do know when I'm being set up," he said knowing full well that he was.

"On the other hand, you should know that all these lines have been written for only you and me," she said, not willing to be sidetracked, her smile shifting slightly as her eyes followed him and studied him.

"That sounds outrageously far-fetched."

"What's more far-fetched?" Emily asked evenly but without mimicking him this time. "That life is merely a collection of random events to which we react, or, alternatively, that we exist within a much greater universe, most of which we know nothing about? You know.... Anyway, you should know by now: layers upon layers, Patrick."

"Other than our ineluctable death, nothing is predetermined," Patrick quickly said while wondering where Emily might be going with this. "God, if indeed, there is a God, does not write our lines for us. We are the product of circumstances and our free will. Other than that, nothing is guaranteed – nothing ordained; pure chance guides our lives."

Emily threw back her head and laughed. "Ha! I knew I could get you going!"

Patrick shook his head, once again trying not to smile. He sat back to gather his thoughts, continuing to study her, mesmerized by her.

"And you're quite wrong too!" Emily added, her eyes shining as they followed Patrick's shifting expression. "How are our lives any different from the predetermined course of Earth about the sun, the decay of an atom?"

"We understand those things. We can mathematically model them to great precision."

"Oh yeah, right!"

Emily laughed again, lightly; not laughing at Patrick but with him.

THE SECOND FIRST TIME

"I don't like the cold. I feel it all the time, you know; right down to my core. I can't get warm; I can never seem to get warm. Why do you think that is?"

"It is symptomatic of your illness."

"Maybe."

There's always some warmth in even the most penetrating cold. It is theoretically impossible to reach a point where there is absolutely no warmth, no motion. Minus two hundred seventy-three point one five degrees Celsius is a theoretical point that has never been reached because it cannot exist. Even at the theoretical limit, nature mimics the heart.

"I don't like the cold."

"Nor I."

"Tell me about the first time, then – which is really the second time, I know – but tell me about it anyway."

"I broke almost every ethical law I know to find out who you were, and, later, when I discovered how sick you are, what was wrong with you, I requested your records. They gave them to me."

"Of course, with your reputation, they were only too glad to have you look over my case."

"Yes, that's correct."

"You are quite a talented man, Doctor Marsh. All of this must seem very strange to you."

"It does."

"May I call you Patrick?"

"Yes, you may."

"You may call me Emily."

"Well, thank you very much, Emily."

"Don't mention it."

Patrick watched Emily through the half-open door. Delicate and petite, like an early spring flower just bloomed, all the rich detail of the flower in the shape of her nose and mouth and the curve of her chin leading to small ears pierced with miniature emeralds. Later he would often think back on that version of Emily: how sad, how lonely; but as she had looked up, he again knew they were connected in some way: her sadness, perhaps; his sympathy for her; the mystery of her.

She read out his nametag as he entered. "Doctor Patrick Thomas Marsh; you look too young to be a doctor."

First words.

Patrick had nodded while trying to reconcile the woman before him with the woman in the coffee shop. He might have believed he had only imagined her except that Bekele had seen her too. Odd how things are; reason and logic coupled with faith and hope make us who we are. But now here she was after a long search, the inevitability of them finally meeting culminating in now – not that there was anything in the world that can truly be described as 'inevitable.' She was, however, not what he had expected, even though there was no doubt, none whatsoever, that she was the same woman. He felt the truth of that immediately upon entering the small examining room.

"They asked if I might speak with you," he had said, finding a chair, turning it around and then sitting.

"Whatever for?"

Second words.

He had replied in Italian. "We are of the same age – that is it, mostly."

"You speak Italian," she had replied, also in Italian; she had seemed pleased.

"I try," he'd replied, and they had laughed together.

It was in her file that she was second-generation Italian. He had guessed that she would be able to speak it.

Switching to English, he had asked if she had come alone. She'd answered her father had dropped her off. Her mother was deceased. Very sad. "She left a big hole in our lives, my father's life and mine." Emily tapped her head. "Same illness, you know; it runs in the family." He'd asked if she had any brothers or sisters; the answer, no. Friends? A few, fading fast. Who would want to be the friend of someone who could not remember you, or anything you might have shared together? It was all in her records, but he had asked anyway.

They didn't talk for long, for less than an hour or so. He explained her condition, not that she needed an explanation. The onset of encephalitis brought about by an as yet unknown virus, the encephalitis attacking her memory so that her past was almost entirely removed and her present limited only to a day or two. The diagnosis was called retrograde amnesia, rare but not unknown. Unfortunately, her condition did not end there. Reading the diagnosis of her secondary cancer and the expected prognosis, his heart had sunk. She had months only, if that.

He had called Alessandra again a few nights later looking for some reason for what he was feeling, for that was the real problem since what he thought and felt were two different things. Alessandra asked in return about the possible folds of fate within which her son might be entangled. "As you well know, Patrick, the world is not always as it seems." The darkened room in which he stood warmed, indicating that Alessandra was smiling. She was also teasing him. She added softly, "There is no such thing as fate." She laughed. "Well, you know I am joking about that. But to answer your question, yes, I am quite sure there is a reason that the two of you should meet, or I should say collided like you have. My advice is to follow your heart in this matter, because that is all we have when our intellect and logic fail us." Alessandra often spoke like that, describing the world in her own light, and not taking sides generally.

He had asked Emily how the treatments were going, how she felt, what she felt, and what she thought about as she sat back in the chair undergoing the transfusions. It was not for the encephalitis; her current treatment was designed for the widely distributed micro-fibrous tumors eating at her brain, triggered no doubt by the encephalitis. What we don't know about why the body does this or that could fill volumes.

"I let my mind wander. I try not to think about it ... you know."

"Yes, I think so."

The mind is a strange place; it does strange things and goes to strange places; it needs discipline to function properly. Patrick had spent his lifetime developing that discipline, but, still, he could not let up, not even for a moment; to do so would run the risk of betraying his future.

Emily sat upright; she stretched, closed her eyes, and smiled, taking a deep breath, letting it out slowly. Opening her eyes, she turned to him and said, "This is funny... You're going to think me crazy."

"Why is that?"

She mused. "Hmmm...." She shook her head.

"I'd like to hear."

"I often think of our summer cottage," she said opening her eyes to find him. "The water is so clear you can see the bottom twenty feet below and see fish halfway up meandering through waving strands of weed. Sometimes I can feel the cool waters on my flesh, silky and smooth. I like that sensation more than any other; it is like breathing. Sometimes I lay back and pretend I'm floating, letting the waves carry me up and down...."

"It sounds wonderful – sublime, even."

"It is a special, pristine place."

"I can see what you described in my mind – you have painted it beautifully."

"When I feel like that, I sometimes slip into another reality, a world I see only in the far distance," she added, turning to find him. "It is a village held in the embrace of mountains. No one can get to it, you see. It is quite far away, the passes impenetrable by the uninitiated. I see a woman, older but very attractive. She could be my mother, I think. But I don't have a mother, at least I don't remember one, although I know that everyone has a mother, don't they? I just cannot remember mine. It is sad, isn't it?"

She hesitated.

"In dreams?" Patrick prompted. "Or while you are awake?"

"Yes, yes, that's right: in dreams; I am transported there in my dreams. It's always in color, too – brilliant color.... Do you ever dream in color?"

"Often."

"I don't know what it is about, dreaming in color; it makes everything so... more. Do you know what I mean by 'more'?"

"I think so."

"Anyway, I don't know about your dreams, but it's always an amazing 'hurt your eyes' kind of color in mine. The grass is an amazing, an almost effervescent, brilliant green cast across the hillsides, thick like a carpet; impossible flowers – red, gold, purple, blue, pink, white, yellow, reach up to the sunlight. Do you know what I mean by 'impossible'? I think I told you all about impossible."

"Yes I do."

Emily laughed lightly. "If you want to know impossible, know that the flowers dance in the sunlight," she said, returning to her vision.

It is not unusual for someone in Emily's condition, with the damage her brain had already sustained, to have visions of this nature.

"I know what you are thinking; you're thinking I'm crazy and should be locked up," Emily said. She mimicked the head nurse, shifting her tone, imitating her French accent. "Have her day pass revoked, Doctor Marsh!" Patrick reached across and held Emily's hand to settle her. She was flying, almost hyperventilating. The drugs she had been given were responsible. Amobarbital. Too much of it.

Emily caught her breath but then continued, some part of her, the part of her not spinning her tale, watching him carefully. "Of course, there is a dark and deep river," she added soberly, but she then frowned, looking down then glancing up at him. She lifted her chin. "There is always a dark and deep river in these sorts of things, isn't there?"

"I know a place by a river," Patrick admitted in response. It just fell out of him.

Emily leaned back, mildly surprised. "You do?"

"Alessandra told me all about her famous river in her made up stories of winter and spring. Silly tales for children."

"Who is Alessandra?"

"My mother."

She looked at him suspiciously and then looked away and blushed deeply, the pallor of her nearly translucent flesh unexpectedly transforming into a healthy sheen. He felt for her pulse; it was skipping along.

"How are you feeling?"

"I'm all right."

She quietly smiled as the glow slowly dissipated. He shook his head. What was happening? He couldn't guess. He prompted her but she would not continue. She stared straight ahead, her smile not leaving her, keeping it for as long as she could.

Later, when his mind had stopped racing, and when it seemed they had reverted to their expected roles, he had asked her again what she was feeling. She had awakened from wherever she had gone through, the sickly pallor and bottomless weakness that had filled her returning. Her eyes were lowered, half shut. He thought for a moment she might faint and again wondered if she had been given too much Amobarbital. He must check. She was half out of her mind from its effects.

"You mean, inside my head, my illness?"

"Yes, that."

"It feels like I'm drowning or falling." Emily suddenly pitched forward and throwing herself back began to gasp in huge quantities of air as if she had been submerged under water too long. She reached out her hand and he held it to steady her, counting the seconds until she calmed and was breathing normally.

She apologized, wiping her eyes. "Sorry…"

She glanced at him and then quickly away. "Do you know what is wrong with me?" she asked. "You are very young, though; you can't be much of an expert; not enough time." She shifted her eyes back to him and then again away, and blushed glancing back. "I hope you don't think I'm criticizing you," she quietly added, continuing to blush, tipping her head away.

Whatever had caused her to hyperventilate had run its course. Something, some thought; perhaps a nascent memory triggering an autonomous response: the mind–body interface. "No, I don't think that – I know you are speaking honestly. I am a fully qualified neurologist, but I know I still have a lot to learn. I am here to study under Dr. Ansari; he is one of the world's leading experts. I am very fortunate."

"I know him, I think. He's a bigwig around here, isn't he? He seems nice. He has kind eyes. He cares."

"You met him just this morning. I walked in a few moments after he left."

Emily hesitated as this sank in. It was not a surprise; lapses of her short-term memory were common and understood by her.

"So do you and he know what's wrong with me?" she asked quietly; "I mean, we all know, don't we, but can you and the great what's his name – I can't remember; it is silly, isn't it; you said his name just now; I remember that – think of a cure, something we can do? I don't want to take a trip down that river, now, do I?"

Patrick shook his head and agreed with her. He went on to say what he needed to say and what Emily had been told on multiple occasions, but he would explain it all again for her sake. "You have a rare type of cancer growing in your brain. We think it is congenital, in that you were born with it and it is now beginning to grow, triggered, we believe, by the encephalitis you suffered from earlier. It is like a thousand mini blood clots spread out in a fibrous mass throughout your hippocampus. It affects your memory both short term and long, but mostly long term. The tendrils, for that is what they are, tendrils, and it is why they are so difficult to eradicate, also extend into your temporal lobe, the region through which the hippocampus communicates with the rest of the cerebral cortex, which in turn affects the way you perceive the world. You have visions. Like the mountains, the flowers. They seem very real, I know. But we should be able to do something about that, mitigate them somehow. I have some ideas. They are proven techniques."

"The river – you forgot the river," she offered as her only comment, studying him, searching for some other meaning to what he was saying.

"Yes, and the river."

"Again."

"Yes, again."

"The river."

"Yes, the river."

She hesitated. "So I'm a total goner," she said, waving the notion aside in a way that suggested she really did not believe it.

How many times can one be doomed before one does

not believe in one's demise anymore, Patrick wondered. "There are a number of things we can try still," he said instead. "Dr. Ansari and I have been coming up with a strategy. We have—"

She interrupted him. "I meant my memory. You see, I don't know who I am. I have no past, and if you have no past are you anything at all? That is more important, don't you think? I mean, each day, I live with nothing, no past, no future. Time has abandoned me. Here, look!" She rolled up the sleeve. Her forearm was emboldened in notes written by her so that she would remember: names, times, places, in blue ink and black, sometimes red, with whatever pen might be handy. They began at her wrist, wrapped around the circumference of her arm up to her elbow. She showed him her other arm; it was the same. She stated flatly, "I don't remember writing any of this, but it was me; I did it. It is my hand-writing."

He had been unaware of the markings on her arm; someone should have told him.

"You are the illustrated woman," he said.

"What's that supposed to mean?"

He thought through his response, shifting the direction. "The lettering on your arm is meant to enlighten – do you have more anywhere else?"

"All over." She showed him her other arm again, then her leg. She lifted her blouse.

He examined her arm closely, running his fingers gently over the markings before letting his hand fall away. "You will always be Emily no matter what you remember or do not remember," he said finally, looking up. "Do you not feel like yourself?"

"Yes, of course, I feel like myself! Who else would I

be?"

"But have we met before?" Emily suddenly asked, her temperament suddenly switching, almost fearful. "Tell me I didn't forget you! It just occurred to me that maybe I have! How embarrassing if true!"

"This is the first time," Patrick said slowly, taking her hand again, calming her. "But I did see you from a distance not too long ago in the coffee shop downstairs on the main Mezzanine. You sat at a table by the window: blue coat, red scarf, your hair tied back, a diamond barrette, and emerald earrings. You ordered hot chocolate capped with marshmallows."

"You were watching me."

"So I was."

"Ah, so this is not the first time! This is the second time! I knew it!" She grasped his arm and smiled, excited. "But that doesn't sound like me, does it? I mean, not drinking the hot chocolate! I love hot chocolate especially, particularly with marshmallows – and I do love that barrette! I'm not wearing it today. I must have seen you!"

"You gave no indication that you might have."

She laughed. "Tell me we're not married!"

"We are not."

"Lovers?"

He shook his head.

Her smile opened. She tipped her head. The quick change in her was remarkable, Patrick thought. He wondered what might have triggered it.

"But I did see you, I'm sure of it," she said confidently, keeping her eyes on him. They shone brightly.

"Where did I sit?"

"Pardon?"

"Where did I sit?"

"I don't know what you mean."

"The coffee shop off the Mezzanine."

"Oh!"

"The hot chocolate with marshmallows."

"Oh, yes, I remember now. Sorry. I lost the thread there a bit. It happens. I did not realize I had. Lost it, I mean." She took a deep breath. "I feel quite normal now."

She was floating. "I was sitting with my brother," he said.

"Ah, you have a brother! I know a lot about you already! You have a mother and brother! And I do love that diamond barrette!" She touched her hair. "I'm not wearing it today. And those earrings; I love them too; they were my grandmother's; she gave them to me before she died. Her name was Ruth – everyone called her Ruthie; her last name was Wilson: Ruthie Anne Wilson. See, I can remember some things!"

She leaned forward, her temperament shifting again. Her voice lowered. "You know, I think you might be the one who will save me, I really do. You could be, you know. You have come from the distance of your life to meet me now. Do you believe that sort of thing? I do. I believe you are here to give me back my life. There is a good possibility, don't you think?"

"I hope to. I hope to make it better."

She thought, looking away, and then back, back to herself. "I just don't want to die as a nobody, you see; that would be the worst. I wouldn't even know who I am when I died. You wouldn't let that happen now, would you?"

"Not if I can help it."

"You can stop that from happening, can't you?"

"I hope to."

He had almost held her in his arms, the empathy he felt for her was so strong. He was shocked he would consider doing such a thing; she was a patient; he could lose his license for the suggestion of the possibility. Even so, she apparently held that power over him. As it was, he held her hand throughout what remained of their session. She seemed unaware that he was doing so, and that, in itself, puzzled him. She was a woman of contrasts, he realized, her mind a tumble of emotion and images all brought about by the unusual growth in her brain. He, on the other hand, was, well... uncharacteristically overtaken. Already he was quite out of control and he knew it.

"Do you know what strikes me about that second-first time?" Emily asked in his office, the window overlooking the St Lawrence and the mid-winter scene. She answered. "I did not know what you could possibly see in me." She turned to face him. "But I know you do see something in me, or we wouldn't be sitting her talking like this now, would we?"

"Are you suggesting I like you in some other way other than just liking you, which, of course, I do?"

"I am – do you have a problem with that?"

He shook his head and shrugged.

"But tell me one of your stories, please," she said.

"We are supposed to be talking about you," Patrick answered gently, reminding her.

"I like your stories better, and it is pretty obvious why. Because I am an empty shell, that's why, and what you tell me fills in a lot of holes that used to be filled but are no longer. I am empty, empty...."

When he did not respond right away, instead looking

away as if what she had said pained him, she indicated Patrick's cheek, the remains of a scar, barely discernible.

"What's this?" Emily asked, tracing the outline as it would be on her cheek, regaining his full attention.

"A sunburn I suffered a few years back."

"You should watch that, you know; bad sunburns can cause skin cancer later on in life."

He raised his shoulders, letting them drop as if it didn't matter.

"It doesn't look like that kind of scar, frankly. But tell me all about your life, please. We can come back to that scar thing later. Tell me all about Alessandra especially. I am all ears."

"My mother? Why?"

"She's the key, know you."

"The key to what?"

"All of this." Emily indicated the office and the world beyond the boundary of the window. She sat back. "But speak slowly, I have to take notes." She laughed but then extended her hand, which after a brief hesitation, he accepted.

"I know you like me," she repeated.

"Do you think?"

Emily nodded and smiled. "Huh, huh." She drew his hand to her, holding it in both of hers. "And don't leave anything out."

PATRICK HAS A BROTHER

Patrick Thomas Marsh has a brother whose name is Bekele Amara Okello; but what is in a name: to Patrick, everything.

"You have a brother?"

"I definitely have a brother."

"Tell me about him then."

Patrick Thomas Marsh has a brother whose name is Bekele Amara Okello; but what is in a name; to Patrick, everything.

"Why everything?"

"Listen."

The dust devils of the great desert leapt up to lick his calves and then lifted higher to fill his nose and mouth and sting his eyes – sift through his hair, slip down the length of his back. With each step, there was another and then another spiral, each spinning up from the scorched earth as if each step he took somehow triggered the mystery that agitated beneath. It was 1984, and Patrick stood with his father in the town of Korem, Ethiopia. Death was all around them. Patrick was five years old.

The whirl of dust; the sea of heat. The searing sun and light. The deep and shrill sounds, and the dark faces looking up from where they lay. The angry soldiers and the white men in their white vans and their cameras. The desiccating dryness and stench of human faeces and death.

"My God, I should not have brought you!" Francesco cried as he drew Patrick close, turning him against the billowing folds of his shirt. "Don't look! Oh my God!"

Patrick remembered the sensation of the soft fabric

against his cheek and knew that this was how Francesco hoped to shield him from the suffocating incomprehensibility of an insane world.

"You are too young for this, my son! I am sorry, I am sorry!"

The famine was at its peak. Ultimately, one million human beings would perish, their bodies returning to the greater landscape. The rains had not come for two consecutive years, but that was not the true reason the people starved. There was war. Farming had stopped, desperately needed food supplies had been commandeered, and it was not safe to move on the roads. The men in Addis Ababa ordered it. The men who held the guns ensured it. The men and women and children who had no voice and no choice died because of it.

"We forget who we are when we allow such things," Francesco had said when they felt they could remember.

Then, moving off to the side toward the periphery where the observers and diplomats could safely gather, his voice ringing in Patrick's memory like epic poetry, Francesco explained, "This is how we too often come into the world, Patrick: out of war and atrocity."

He had only been a child but from this point forward, the real world would be held up against this day, the memory of it a wound that could never be healed only placated by the assiduous application of love. It is a true thing; it is certain: if there was anything in his life Patrick did possess, it was love. It was freely given, without strings, and powerful enough to stop time and fold it back upon itself, ensuring the past was always present.

"You may not remember any of this, Patrick," Francesco had explained at the time. "But this is what we do. It is not a legal thing...." He thought a moment before kneeling next to Patrick, Patrick momentarily blinded by the sun over Francesco's shoulder. "We have thought long and hard on what this life means," Francesco continued, each syllable colored by the sand, "and have decided that, if we can, each of us, do one good thing, lift one small life out of just one of the many hells that exist on this Earth, then we can, perhaps, accomplish something meaningful; we hope so anyway." Patrick again pressed his face against his father's shirt as the voice he remembered so clearly echoed through time and place. "The idea that that might be so gives us reason, and a right, we believe, to continue in our privileged lives."

In those far-flung days, half imagined perhaps though still burned into his memory, Alessandra spoke in the intertwining threads of his memory for the first time, her voice a study of metrical poetry that filled the spaces between the cacophonies of life with the sound of golden bells on silver threads. "We believe this with all our heart," she said, making their lives all true and right, with Francesco adding, "After today, Patrick, you shall have a brother."

"'We believe this with all our heart'.... God, I love that woman!" Emily sighed, sitting back, shaking her head, running her hands through her hair.

Patrick smiled.

"Francesco, too; he was a good man. I'm sorry he died and left you like he did and so soon – not his fault, of course."

Patrick nodded.

"It is in my journal – it is written right here." She showed him, holding the journal up. "But how can you remember this so well, it was so long ago?" she asked, setting it aside.

"I don't, not really, but I have been told of it so often it becomes like a memory."

"Maybe it's not true at all, then.... Ever think of that?"

"No, not really."

"You should."

"But why would my mother or Francesco lie?"

"Who says they are?"

Memories, true and false, distort the truth of our existence. Not that there is any solid truth to be had; there is no such thing as unbiased "truth" in our minds, nor within our reason, and particularly not in our hearts, Patrick knew.

Perhaps his memories of the famine were not true at all, Patrick thought later when he was a full-grown man who saw so clearly in so many ways and had already learned so much. Memory is malleable, perhaps created out of the myth of the past or created from years sitting at the dinner table across from his brother who looked so different and with a name that was so different. They came from years of listening to Francesco and Alessandra explaining to anyone who might be curious why he and his brother kept the names they were given at birth. "You are Patrick Thomas Marsh, and you," Francesco sometimes announced, just for the fun of it – he was great fun, Francesco, notwithstanding the more serious moments that he always recognized and never trivialized – "you, my boy, are named, not by me but by those who had the right to do so, Bekele Amara Okello!" He would sigh and shrug his shoulders. "But what is in a name, you might ask? I shall tell you what's in a name – everything! If you cannot say who you are, who are you?" he demanded to know.

Occasionally, just to be certain Patrick had it exactly right, Francesco would remind him with the possibility of a test later, "Patrick Thomas Marsh, Alessandra, the love of my life and whom I have known forever, has told me she found you alone in the back of a lorry in the midst of the collapse of Southern Rhodesia. Such a beautiful place, beautiful, beautiful but with so much horror and so much sad history. She told the driver she would look after you and love you, and he willingly gave you to her, even though he had been unable to find your name from a long list of names, after comparing it to the number on your back. He believed, without proof, you were called Patrick. No one complained or suggested it was not right or legal for her to take you – kidnapping, you know; sort of. But who to talk to? Who to tell? No one cared; such it was then in what is now called Zimbabwe. But what number, you ask, was pinned to your back? Well, it was...let me see...and I have to take Alessandra's word on this because I was not there...yes, the number was forty-two! No, that's not a joke! Remove that smile from your face, Patrick Thomas Marsh!

"And just to be absolutely clear, this is your brother, Bekele Amara Okello," Francesco would go on unable to stop but now laughing. "He is an Amharic Ethiopian whom we discovered alone and starving in the highlands of Tigray, in the town of Korem, in a land from which mankind originated many millennia ago; the woman at whose feet he sat told us his name. I did not have to ask her twice; she practically shouted it out! She wanted the world to know!"

"Now that part is true!" Alessandra exclaimed from

the counter, preparing their dinner, laughing with them. "Patrick and Bekele listen to only half of what your father says! Whatever he says is bull, all bull! It is all in his silly mind!"

In response and in all seriousness, Francesco would turn to himself, place his hand across his chest as if outraged, and say, "And just to be clear, I am Francesco Adolfos Tosselli, obviously Italian - from my name anyway; some people can't believe it..." He would let his explanation trail off as he waited, ready, for Alessandra to challenge him.

Alessandra, unwilling to take the bait, would invariably roll her eyes. "You are fascinated with everything Italian, Francis, but you are no more Italian than I am! Tell the truth for once!"

Francesco, aghast, would exclaim, "Truth! What is truth? I thought we agreed not to tell them the truth! The truth; oh, yes, the truth: the truth when it does not set you free often sets you upside down! To hell with truth! And I won't change my name for anyone! This is who I am! Look carefully and pay attention! Francesco Adolfos Tosselli! This is me! To relieve all doubt, I carry an Italian passport which says who I am and let me tell you there is no greater authority than an Italian passport!"

Immediately putting his passion aside, he would proceed to present Alessandra, as if presenting the world with a wonderful gift. His voice mellow, and dreamy, slowly increasing in intensity. "And this lovely creature my boys, is Alessandra and your mother! I have known her all my life so I can vouch for whom she claims to be, and, oh, and if you hadn't guessed, she wears the pants around here! I do and say everything she tells me to, or else!"

Turning back to Alessandra he'd exclaim, "And you are ruining the story, my love! Let me have my fun!"

Alessandra had said, "You like to tell stories, there is no doubt about that, but at our expense! But the boys don't require a name to tell them who they are, Francis! We are who we are! We prove it every day, do we not? Do we lie about ourselves, or are the lies who we are?"

Patrick had known for many years that Francesco's real name was Francis – at least that is what Alessandra called him – but his father would never answer to it. He would instead reach for Alessandra as she floated across the room, catching then wrapping her up in his arms, kissing her check and neck as she squirmed, laughing, to get away. Inevitably free, halfway across the room, she would turn back and bow low from her waist, her dark hair spilling about her as she laughed.

"Alessandra Elizabetta Marsh at your service!"

Emily jumped up from the table and bowed low from her waist. "Emily Martina Portinari at your service!" She pointed at Patrick. "I won't change my name for anyone either! This is who I am! Look carefully and pay attention, Doctor Marsh! Emily Martina Portinari! This is me!"

She laughed, laughing as Alessandra had laughed, then returned to her chair, and sitting, returning a loose strand of hair behind her ear, pinning it place again with the barrette that shone in the overhead light.

"God, I love Alessandra!" She sighed again. "And you noticed she has the same last name as you, right? You are her son."

"I have already admitted that."

"I mean her son, son – her biological son."

"Do you know where you are right now, Emily?"

Patrick asked, refusing to be baited. His pen hovered as if he was about to take a note. He had not taken a single note yet.

"Why, do you think I don't know where I am – or more important, who I am, or who you might be?"

"Just answer the question, please."

Emily straightened in the chair, settled, and then looked about. "I am on the top floor of my father's house sitting across from you at this old table I inherited from my grandmother. You are Doctor Patrick Thomas Marsh…. God knows a brilliant man. But you always address yourself using your full name. It is interesting. Does Bekele? He only goes by Bekele, doesn't he, and Alessandra only by Alessandra? I know this – I don't know why I know this, but I do…. And put the pen down, there's no need. I keep the journal around here." She smiled.

Patrick put the pen down.

"I thought this was about your brother?" she said after a moment of reflection and silence between them.

"You are right."

"A little more focus on your part then, please." Emily laughed aloud, throwing her head back. "Ha!"

"What was that?"

"I laughed. That's, 'Ha!'" Emily laughed again, her laugh flying out of her like a shot, "Ha!" She waited for Patrick's response, smiling and when he did not respond, prodded. "You're turning red! I thought I was the only one who did that!" She laughed again, but quietly this time, directing her laughter inward. "Sorry if you find me a bit much." She prodded him again, waving him onward. "Keep going," she said softly, sitting back, keeping her smile, tipping her head. "Please."

"No one would ever suspect you are brothers but there is no one under heaven who can doubt that you are." That is what Alessandra said almost every night just as she was tucking them in and about to kiss them good night.

Alessandra turning out the light, silhouetted against the setting sun.

"Patrick and Bekele....?"

Their heads turning toward her.

"Thank this world for each other."

"Yes, Mama."

"Yes, Mama."

It was true what heaven knew, for when Bekele, Patrick's brother who was not a brother, breathed, Patrick breathed; and when Bekele turned his head, Patrick turned his. They cried together, laughed together, and ate breakfast, lunch, and dinner together, sitting across from Francesco and Alessandra who sat side by side. Alessandra, lovely in the light cast through the window, her voice level and soft and full of love, would speak of the day as if it had been one of the most important of their lives. She would get up from the table to serve the dish, her dress following the shape of her as she danced across the floor. She would smile and sing, returning to refill their glasses, stack more food, or clear the plates.

Once she said – and Patrick remembered this only in retrospect, years and years later and only when reminded by Emily – "I wish you boys had a sister! She'd be pretty and happy. I'd give her dancing lessons and she'd wear a flower-patterned dress."

"Like the one you're wearing?" he had asked.

"Yes, just like this one, only smaller, prettier too, made of cotton with patterns of golden poppy and peony, tied about her waist with a bow! Her blonde hair would be pulled back behind her ears and tied in place with a barrette."

"What's a barrette?"

"It's a clip that holds a woman's hair in place; hers would be made up of diamonds... not real diamonds, they'd just look like diamonds!"

"What would you call her?"

"I'd call her Emily... A good Italian name!" she would add and laugh, glancing at Francesco and blushing a little.

"Ha! I have heard this before!" Emily exclaimed.

"Where, I wonder?"

"You, of course! Don't you remember? Look! It is not in my journal – I just remembered it!" She raised her hand. "Hold on! I will write it down!"

They cleaned up together, Francesco washing, Patrick drying; Bekele helping to put away. When Bekele was tall enough to reach the cupboards, Alessandra would retreat to the living room and put her feet up. She would bow herself out of the kitchen, adding a flourish but not before reaching up to kiss Francesco tussle Patrick's hair, and give Bekele a quick hug. They never spoke while doing the dishes; they always listened to the music she played: Vivaldi and Bach, always Vivaldi and Bach, nothing else.

"Bach... Do you like Bach?" Emily asked.

"Yes, of course. Why do you ask?"

"Because Alessandra likes Bach."

From Addis Ababa, they found themselves in Cairo; from Cairo to Tel Aviv; from Tel Aviv to New Delhi; from New Delhi to London – and then finally, mysteriously even, a return to Addis Ababa. Bekele was seventeen years old, Patrick nineteen; it was the year Patrick left to study philosophy at Sapienza, Universita di Roma, where he would learn what it is to be Italian. He graduated with honors in two years and then transferred to King's College, London, to study medicine, and from there a brief sabbatical at the Faculty of Medicine at McGill, Montreal. He changed there, in Montreal; it was within that cold city he finally met Emily, the real Emily.

"I like that – the real Emily."

"Are you not real?"

"I think so... I feel real."

"Then you are."

"If you say so... but I'm not too sure even if you are, given everything." She tapped her head.

"Give me a break...."

"Ha!" Emily laughed but then quickly quieted. She asked, "When did Francesco die and what did he die of?"

"While I was up at King's College, and he died in an accident while he and Alessandra were away. He died instantly. He hit his head on the ice. You never know, do you?"

"I cannot imagine how Alessandra must have felt. What did she do after?"

"She came home, with his ashes. It was too expensive to bring his body back, and too expensive for myself and Bekele to go all the way to where he died – somewhere in the midst of the mountains somewhere in British Columbia, Canada; thousands and thousands of kilometres away, days of air travel. I think they might have gone home to visit but I'm not entirely certain; Alessandra never really said or spoke of where they lived or their days there. She avoided the subject and even to this day I am not sure why. Except in fairy tales, of course; she would describe her home in fairy tales. Mad and impossible stories – I have told you some of them already; check your journal. But I do know this: Francesco was not Italian; he just liked to think he was or tell others he was Italian. Of course, he worked a whole career with the Italian diplomatic corps, so it was conducive to his employment that the Italians believed it. I am quoting him on that. He did not always make up stories; Francesco spoke the truth more often than not, in his own way."

Patrick recalled Francesco joking about his tendency to exaggerate. "You will have to excuse me, but I just find my real self so boring, that's all."

"In another life, then?"

"Yes, in another life."

"Francesco spoke eight languages as far as I know, and perhaps more," Patrick went on to explain. "A whole host of dialects, Amharic and Oromo not the least of them. He taught me many of them. He apparently, although it has never been said explicitly, grew up in the same village as Alessandra, and where Alessandra has returned to and lives now in her childhood home. She moved back a month or so after Francisco's funeral. They are both Canadian; I am Canadian, too, but not Bekele; he stayed with his nationality. Francesco and Alessandra were childhood sweethearts. Never married; although they claimed they were married; in their hearts, they said. Married by their hearts, as Alessandra liked to say." Patrick smiled, remembering.

"I like that. I dream of the mountains still, you know. But keep going with your life story; I want to hear more."

Flying home, Bekele had the window seat; after all, it was to his ancestral home they were returning after stints in London, Rome, Johannesburg, Tel Aviv. Patrick leaned in close. Thirty-thousand feet below lay the inspired blue of the Red Sea cut by the razor-sharp shoreline of Djibouti. The aircraft pulled them forward and the landscape broke apart and morphed into the hopeless and golden emptiness of the Danakil and the blinding white and cyan of *Abhe Bad.* This was the meeting point of three sliding landmasses: Africa, Arabia, and India, a place where near-continuous earthquakes split the Earth's crust and opened rifts that would eventually tear the Afar from Africa like a page from a book. He leaned across Bekele, pressing his face against the plastic window to find the volcanic cauldrons. The volcanoes belch their poisonous gases and molten rock into the world of man, into one of the hottest and driest places on Earth from an even greater hell sourced from the unimaginable forces only a world that orbits a sun can create.

Bekele pushed past him and pointed.

"Look at that!"

"Look at what?"

"That!"

Patrick again leaned in, pressing his face against the plastic, this time holding his breath so as not to fog the pane.

Bekele explained. "Look at the land; the Afar carry the salt across all that – long lines of camels. It has been the same for thousands of years; nothing has changed, nothing ever changes in the *Danakil*."

Patrick freed the window as Bekele leaned in again and continued, speaking through the plastic window to the desert below. "I belong down there," he said his voice quieting. Adding in awe, he said, "That is my home."

That was the way Bekele was that year. It was not good enough to be Bekele Amara Okello; he wanted to know what that really meant.

"We should go then," Patrick said, glancing at Bekele, surprised by him, knowing him then for the first time. To know something like that, to know where one belongs, that is something, he had thought.

"You're right, that is something."

Patrick quietly nodded.

"I like Bekele. You must love him very much."

"I do. He is my best friend."

"Lucky.... Do you many friends?"

"No, not really."

In the same home they had left almost fifteen years earlier, the brothers stood in their trellised garden surrounded by courts of peacock gladiolus, purple iris, and strings of falling clematis. They stood beneath the waning bloodless moon suspended in the stark sky of central Ethiopia. Francesco Alfonso Tosselli stood with them. He was always with them. It was where he wanted to be, he said, nowhere else.

He listened to the boys talk and plan. Content, happy, he swirled the wine in his glass, holding the nearly translucent red liquid up against the evening sky. He returned it to his nose, carefully inhaled the deep bouquet, and then sat back on the stone steps and again swirled, spinning the glass faster and faster, watching the wine lift dangerously close to the rim. He suddenly stopped and waited for the dark liquid to settle before taking another sip. The brothers, his sons, joined him on the steps, sitting above and to each side, waiting for him to speak on anything other than how delicious the wine was...the wonderful, rich color, the subtlety of its bouquet...hint of raspberry.... He suddenly tossed the last of the wine back; a trickle escaped from his mouth and ran down the length of his chin, making the boys laugh. He smiled, choking slightly as he wiped away the excess with the back of his hand. He set the glass aside and then climbed to his feet, placing a hand on each of their shoulders.

He looked from Bekele to Patrick, and then back to Bekele. "Okay...you're going, Bekele," he announced, "but Patrick is going with you." He waited for his final word to sink in before adding, "Now move over, your old man is coming in for a landing!"

He squeezed between the two, placing an arm about each, drawing them inward. The boys laughed but then quieted as he quieted. Together they sat within the peaceful softness of the evening, watching and listening, smelling and feeling the timelessness of the moment, each conscious of the wondrous silence, the warm air, the scented flowers, and the close presence of one another: the moon, the stars, and all those infinite places beyond.

"God, you were lucky!"

Patrick nodded.

"And Francesco, was he always like that?"

"Yes, he was. He had a great sense of humour, and quite a jokester. I often wish I was as strong as him." Patrick placed his hand over his heart to show what he meant.

"You're not strong?"

"Not always."

"You seem very strong to me."

THE MYSTERY OF US

Patrick pressed his fingertips against the cold glass of the window and leaned inward catching his reflection – dark hair, dark eyes, white skin – overlaying the bleak winter day falling toward night. The touch was cold; the scene was colder. A biting and bleak winter of grey skies: leafless trees and filthy snow. The slope that falls toward the theoretical limit of absolute zero leads to stillness, absolute, near perfect, stillness. He stared into his own eyes and again felt the chill of loneliness and emptiness that haunted him, and then stepped back and turned away.

Patrick knew death; it was his profession. He had witnessed it in the desert and on the great desert plains of the *Danakil* to say nothing of the countless souls he had shepherded over to the other side in hospital beds in England and now Canada. Today he had seen the pantomime of it in Emily; she had only weeks, perhaps only days, to live: a sudden spasm, unconsciousness, followed by loss of body function, finally unable to breathe on her own; and then, quickly, death. The reason was growing in her head: a living parasite in her brain. His experience told him her ultimate surrender was as inevitable as the sun rising, flying across the sky, and then setting. Emily is the sun, he thought; she is falling down the sky.

At some point during the session Emily had said, "You don't smile much, do you Doctor Marsh?"

"No, I'm afraid not," he had replied and then did smile.

Then she had smiled again, her eyes meeting his.

Patrick pushed himself along the hall, stepping out

quickly. Time marched on drawing him along with it: time, the independent variable of all things, making a mockery of all things, the inevitable demise of the sun as well as an individual's life. He fit Emily's file under his arm and increased his stride, intent on finishing his rounds and going home, such as it was – he had no home in this cold land – but his mind kept returning to her.

Emily was slipping away, even though she dreamed the dreams Alessandra had told, even though she dreamed what he dreamed. With this, he felt a weakness in his legs and his heart twist as he again realized that, but for the grace of God, she was no more than his living, breathing self. It was he, he realized, who was slipping into the broiling sea, floating within the fathomless depths, belly up, eyes open but staring vacantly, spiralling down and down through the eternal current, finally finding a place to rest upon the black and stagnant mud.

"The first breath, the first beating of the heart, is a pact with God," Alessandra had once told him. "And with that first breath there is a connection to the past and the future, the resounding beauty and the heartless horror, and all we do not understand in between."

"And all we do not understand," Patrick said aloud into the empty corridor, feeling the unspeakable reality of the surrounding hallways with the fluorescent lights and the polished floor become less and less tangible, not because it really was, he realized, but because he felt it was. He realized, too, that feeling something changes nothing. Reality is in no way aligned to what one feels.

Patrick's logical mind could imagine life as one great crapshoot with traceable cause and effect and an underlying deterministic structure that mocks us all. In this worldview, the experience of life is not meaningless any more than it is meaningful. Being alive and conscious is merely a monumental coincidence; being dead is the normal state of things. There is nothing to weep for, just as there is nothing to celebrate. There is no Hell or Heaven, no Satan, and no God. We exist in the natural world, all of that and no more: stars and galaxies, yellow suns and blue worlds, mountains, plains, and the blue, blue, almost empty oceans of Earth.

"What are our lives' all about? Why are we here?" he had once asked Alessandra.

Alessandra set her coffee aside, shrugged her slender shoulders, and looked up, closing her eyes against the warming rays of sunlight pouring in through the open window. A quiet smile lifted the corners of her mouth. "The mystery is everywhere you look," she had explained. "In the stars and galaxies, yellow suns and blue worlds, mountains, plains, and everywhere within the blue, blue, almost empty oceans of Earth."

"Do you believe in God?" he had asked, not intending to press his point; it had just slipped out.

Alessandra had looked at him steadily, not answering immediately but then saying, "You have the evidence of your heart to tell you what is true and what is not, Patrick. What does your heart tell you?"

"I can't say, I can't say...."

Alessandra sighed and slowly nodded. "Ah yes, that is part of it, isn't it? Where are the words that cannot be said?" She had picked her next words carefully, taking another moment before answering. "I believe we all speak to God in our own way whether we think we do or not." She indicated the morning sunlight. "Sometimes through the simplest things like sunlight streaming through the window. It is the mystery of us, don't you think?"

Patrick stopped his progress along the hall to once again examine Emily's file. He fumbled with it, snapped it open, glanced at it, and shoved it back beneath his arm unread. That morning he had learned a new word: *Janjaweed.* It was a new word and not a new word; in translation, *Devils on Horseback*. The Janjaweed recoiled out of humanity from the darkest depths of Africa: the dark, dry, and impossible Sudan. Finding Emily alone in the desert, the Janjaweed would drag her from her protective world kicking and screaming, repeatedly raping her in the dirt until, tired of her, finally putting a bullet through her head. The Janjaweed is the growth that eats away at Emily's mind; the connection is cruel and meaningless death.

It was explained in the late-night news. The camera operator walked the length of the village square, his camera quickly shifting and panning the scene as if he had forgotten his training. The scene shook with his hand as he dwelt on the place where the village had once gathered and traded and talked late into the evening. It revealed the cluttered dead still lying unattended, and the trampled earth colored red. A quick shift and the camera centered on the reporter, a woman with blonde hair pulled back and piercing eyes. Patrick immediately thought, again, of Emily. The reported stared back at the camera without flinching. "What are we if not beasts?" she seemed to be saying without actually saying so.

But Patrick understood this: a day, a week, a month from now the survivors, and there would be survivors because someone always knows and remembers and tells others, would straggle into the refugee station carrying nothing but themselves. They would be given food and a place to sit. They would scrounge from others not so unlike themselves, given clothing and a few utensils and their own piece of plastic with which to build a shelter. The wind, never ending, would snap the untied ends, the hollow and empty sound the only connection to reality amidst tens of thousands of souls. There would be no tears, no moans of anguish, just the silence of the snapping plastic.

But here it is, the great mystery: the next day the survivors would climb out of their beds, place their feet on the earth, and go about their lives. It is the most amazing, the most puzzling, and the most mysterious part of the human experience where meaning is often elusive. We get up each morning only because we have hope in the future. How could Patrick be so certain? Faith, he knew, faith – not so much in God, but in our elusive nature that combines cruelty with meaninglessness, beauty with hope, beasts with angels, and for no reason at all except for what is in our hearts.

"The world sucks sometimes."

"It does."

"But I don't think I have faith like you do," Emily said.

Patrick searched for yet another way to explain the permanence of her disease. If, indeed, what Emily suffered was a disease and not a genetic anomaly; her body and genetic code betraying her. That's what they had been talking about; not the Janjaweed, not death in the desert, men and women as beasts, or Alessandra's wisdom, but Emily's inevitable dissolution months or even weeks from now. There is a pattern to these things, an inevitability with no magic rescue, he had told her, barely able to, but forcing himself to.

"You feel a great deal, Patrick; I feel hollow inside compared to you," Emily replied in response, wiping at her eyes.

"That's not true; cannot be true," he said.

"You don't smile much."

He would not respond.

"But you shouldn't try to help me. I am without hope and there's nothing you can do about that." Her hair fell around her, and when she looked up, her face was streaked with tears. "Why are you sitting over there across from me?" she asked. "Why aren't you sitting next to me, holding my hand?"

"I have, all along," he said; and it was true, he had been.

EMILY – HEART AND MIND

Emily's bed slowly spun beneath her, floating, rudderless. She floated off the end of the dock surrounded by tossed, silvery water, a white summer sky, pink granite, and dark, weather-bent pines. "A pristine beauty" was how she described the summer place of her childhood to all who asked. "It is unsullied and unspoiled; you can see the bottom twenty feet below and fish halfway up meandering through waving strands of weed." Emily could feel the cool waters on her flesh, silky and smooth. If she could once again bathe in those waters, would they cure her? Her legs seemed free of her body; they floated, suspended, as if they were not a part of her. Would the purity of the river, filtered through the great forest surrounding it, draw the poison out of her?

Her bed spun beneath her, dropped, and turned as she watched the grey and sun-scattered waves lift and fall. They were gigantic sea-borne waves and she felt lost in the midst of a dream, her eyes closed, and her mind adrift.

Emily opened her eyes. She wanted to turn her head. She felt compelled to do so but the command she summoned from deep within was ignored; all she could do was remain still with her head resting on the pillow, the sheets pulled up to her neck, the room rising and falling. Her breathing followed the pattern: up, and then down, up.... She pried her lips apart and attempted to call. She lifted a hand...and that worked. She heard his voice.

"Emily..."

She had been expecting this to be a dream, but the voice was real, exquisite and real.

"You are dreaming."

His voice was like a key pressed on a piano heard from a distance.

"This is a dream?"

"Life is a dream."

"It feels so real!"

"But it's not."

Emily began to cry.

"Don't cry."

"Why not?"

"Those who love you will cry with you, and you would not want that."

"You love me?"

Again, the world dissolved and reformed into something possibly true. Emily tried to sit up but again her body refused: promises of the end mercifully broken. Only her body was leaving her, nothing else; only her body, she thought. She tried to tell Patrick but could not.

The room collapsed to a singularity as Patrick was saying, "You have had a severe reaction to the drug that was given to you. We flushed it from your system; you should begin to feel better any time now."

Her world would not stop spinning.

"I do feel better, I do...."

"That's good."

The sound of his voice opened her eyes. She turned her head to find him. "You have a lovely sounding voice... Like music. A piano chord. Soft rain. Like water falling," she managed to say, slowly adding to her list.

He was standing over her, smiling down. "Here you go...," he said. He steadied the glass and let her drink using the straw. He set the glass aside and placed a hand on her forehead; satisfied, he lifted her face up to his and held it cupped in his hands, waiting for their eyes to meet.

"You said you loved me," she said when she eventually found him.

"I did?"

Patrick suddenly went away, and her world became empty, composed of nothing, only void. He returned and held her hand; the pressure of his hand in her hand, flesh on flesh, drew her upward out of the abyss and she was able to breathe.

"Hey.... Where have you been?" Patrick asked when she was breathing regularly.

God, his voice.

"Where would I be? I have nowhere to go." Emily sipped the water, again offered. So cold! How did he keep it so cold? "Not dressed for it, you see?" she added and tried to smile.

Patrick pulled up a chair and sat facing her. He reached for her hand, opened it, and kissed her open palm, then settled back into the quiet peace of the room, ready and expectant of a long conversation but in no rush for it to begin or end any time soon. "What should we talk about today?" he asked, the sound of his voice like running water, gentle and melodious.

Emily sighed. "Tell me, why do you call Alessandra, Alessandra – besides that being Alessandra's name, of course?"

"Alessandra again...." Patrick sighed, echoing Emily's sigh, while watching her breathe, checking her pulse. Satisfied, he linked his fingers through hers. "Is Alessandra all you ever want to talk about? Can't we talk about you?"

Emily smiled. It required some effort. She felt she might be fading again. "I only talk of Alessandra – she is all I will talk about...at least for now."

"But why would you want to?" Patrick asked. "I'm afraid I do not understand."

"Because, she is a good mother, that's why."

"You sound as if you know her."

"I know I have never met her, but you must understand that I love her."

"You love my mother?"

"It is not what you think."

"What should I think?"

"You said you love me – I heard you say it, so don't try to deny it. But it's funny....," Emily inserted before Patrick could respond.

"Why is that?"

"Because I don't have a mother."

"We all have mothers."

"Not me – but I would have liked Alessandra to be my mother – if one can choose one's mother, that is, and I know one cannot."

Patrick gently readjusted a strand of her hair. He wrapped it carefully and precisely behind her ear. "You wear your hair back from your face," he said. "You hold it in place with a barrette and let the ends fall to your shoulders," he said, continuing to study Emily, mesmerized by her but trying not to show it.

"I really like my barrettes – the shiny diamond ones, and the ones with the purple and red garnets. I wear them all the time, whenever I can."

"Despite the reaction you just had, I believe you are slowly getting better," Patrick said, trying to set the right tone. "You remember more. You know who I am every time we meet, which is good. You will be wearing your barrettes again soon, I think."

"I'm getting better?"

"Yes, you are – it is quite uncommon, but we should not question it, I suppose. We should take what we can."

"I don't feel like I'm getting better, or worse for that matter – I feel the same."

She unexpectedly tried to sit up. Patrick helped her and propped a pillow behind her head. She could not sustain her new position and slowly sank back into the folds of the bed.

"Do people die in Alessandra's Village of the Heart?" she asked slowly, carefully, as she settled down, focusing on Patrick's response, her eyes locked on him.

"Why do you call it that?"

"Heart, British Columbia, of course; it is where Alessandra grew up, and Francesco too – he was called Francis then. You told me all about it, remember? They were childhood sweethearts."

"I should stop telling you my life's story. I hope you're not putting it all in your journal." Patrick looked about. "I don't see your journal anywhere about; you must have left it at your father's house."

"I keep forgetting where I put the darn thing. Anyway, I wrote it down here." She showed him her arm where she had written in blue ink: 'Alessandra' followed by 'VOH'. She ignored Patrick's surprise. She was still having difficulty focusing. "But I want to know, do people die in Alessandra's Village of Heart, British Columbia?"

"What an odd question," Patrick said. He hesitated, not wanting to frighten her with the truth. "I thought we agreed you were not to be writing on your arm, or hands, feet, or other parts of your anatomy," he said. "I just had Nurse Kumbahaba clean you up."

"I like her, she's nice: kind, very kind. Dark. Where did you say she came from?"

"Nigeria."

"Nigeria, yes; that's in Africa, isn't it?"

"Yes, it is."

"You know, I'm afraid you might be losing it, Doctor Marsh; I really am."

Patrick's expression shifted; he shrugged.

"Are you losing it?" Emily pressed, not letting him escape.

"I don't believe so – what about you?"

"No, what about you?" Emily still pressed. "I'm worried about you, that's all." Again, she did not wait for his response before asking another question. "So tell me again – and be honest – do people die in Heart, British Columbia?"

"No one lives forever but those who live in Alessandra's village, at least the one Alessandra imagines and has told endless tales of to my brother and me, live a long, long time." He quoted Alessandra, remembering her saying, "But nothing lasts forever; not the mountains, not the river, not the world." He was catching up with the sense of amazement he felt; everything about Emily amazed him.

"So, I would die there too?"

"I would die there. Everyone dies, Emily; everyone. It is a fact of our existence. Our mortality defines us."

"Can accidents kill them? Can they drown?"

"Yes, yes I suppose they can, but not normally."

"They die of cancer? Or a disease like mine?"

"No, not of cancer, nor disease of any kind; there is nothing in Alessandra's imagined world that eats a person from within. Everyone dies of old age, loved and held, firm of body and mind, the way the world should be."

"Tell me more...."

"There is no more to tell."

"The stories Alessandra told you and Bekele, silly; tell them to me. Tell me about the winters."

Patrick hesitated. "The winters are impossible," he said finally, wondering where Emily's mind was going. "It is not unknown to have over forty feet of snow."

Emily again tried to sit up and again failed. She lay back with Patrick's help. "Forty feet! Ha! That is impossible!"

"Not as Alessandra imagined it," Patrick explained more enthusiastically, picking up the storyline as Alessandra used to tell. "You can fly down mountains of snow, hugging the nearly vertical surface, your skis in the powder, moving so fast it takes your breath away."

"I don't ski I'm afraid, but even if I did, I would never do that! I would die of fright! Too fast! I would hit a tree or something!"

"Can you skate?"

"Of course! I'm not very good but I can skate!"

"Well, each and every winter day the villagers gather on the river's ice and skate, forming long chains across the ice until it's dark. They drink hot chocolate by the bucket full."

"With marshmallows?"

"Yes, yes, capped and overflowing with marshmallows."

"Ha! You didn't tell me that before! I love hot chocolate with marshmallows!"

"You remember these conversations…. Why do you have me repeat them?"

"What? Remember what?" She waved him on. "Keep going, keep going! I will explain later – if I can remember." She attempted to laugh and nearly did.

Patrick snapped his fingers. "But winter is over just like that! It is as if someone – Mother Nature; God, perhaps – has thrown a switch. One day it's twenty below but by the next, the snow is gone, the river is flowing freely, and their world is green: a blinding, brilliant green that blankets their world. Flowers are instantly in bloom; the air is warm and scented with apple blossoms and lilac and wild rose."

Emily marvelled. "Tell me more!" she breathed, fully fascinated.

Patrick fell right into it. "I know of a place by a river…," he began but then abruptly broke off.

Emily struggled to lift herself up. "Tell me all you know about the river!" she demanded with her voice raised. She drew herself up into a sitting position struggling to do so.

"Why did you stop?" she asked, as he helped.

He checked her pulse; it was racing. "What's so important about the river?" he asked once he was certain the moment had passed.

"Because it's Alessandra's river, silly," Emily managed to say, trying to compose herself. She required a moment. "We lived in the city, my father and me," she finally said, bringing Patrick's full attention back to her. He had been thinking of the odd association Emily was making with his mother. He would have to be more careful.

"We had a cottage up north, on a lake: bright water, tall trees, granite cliffs," Emily explained.

"It sounds beautiful."

She nodded and added, "It is a special, pristine, place. The water is so clear you can see to the bottom twenty feet down."

"Very beautiful."

"I dream of Alessandra," she said, and she began to drift away.

Patrick called after her. "Hey...."

She was falling again.

Her eyes opened. "I'm trying to cross the river to join her, you see, but can't seem to: no bridge, you see; no ferryman to ferry me across for a small fee."

He checked her pulse again. It was steady.

"I stand on the far bank, the river separating us. My feet are stuck in the mud and high grasses, bulrushes, black darting things... shivers of gold...," Emily said in a whisper. "Alessandra is waving from her porch on the far side. She is wearing a summer dress. It billows about her then falls back into place. The wind – it is a summer wind; warm – climbs the riverbank, tumbling through the grasses, turning over the leaves of the leaning maple and hickory before reaching her."

Patrick called after her again, "Hey...."

She struggled to sit up. Failing, and near panic, she grasped his arm. "I somehow took a wrong turn, you see!" She continued to struggle. "I've never known where I am. I've always been lost!" She began to cry as he lay her back.

"You're right here with me."

She shook her head violently back and forth, denying it. "No...!"

Patrick had no idea where all this could be coming from. The mind is a strange land.

Emily pinched her eyes shut. When she opened them, she was back, and calmer. "We're connected, aren't we?" she said evenly.

"Yes, of course."

"By the spirit?"

"Yes, by the spirit."

"You and Alessandra and me?"

Patrick started.

"We have the same soul then, Alessandra and me?" Emily asked.

Patrick looked away so she would not see what swept through him. "Yes, that's right," he said, returning.

"Do you know why?"

"No, I'm afraid not."

She beckoned Patrick near. He leaned in. She whispered in his ear. "Patrick...?"

"I'm here...."

She nodded to the glass on the table and Patrick held it for her as she sipped. The ice had all but melted. The soft coolness seemed to sooth her.

"You lived in Africa?" Emily asked after a moment, her voice trailing, the urge to sleep gaining strength, her body beginning to surrender to it.

"Yes.... Bekele and I were raised in Addis Ababa. I think of Addis Abba as home – it is where Bekele and I grew up. I told you all this more than once. It is in your journal. Please do not inscribe it on your arm."

"You have a brother."

Patrick did not respond; it was not a question.

"Bekele," she added, naming him.

"Yes, Bekele – you remember; that's good."

"It is on this arm." She showed him. Red ink for the left arm: port and starboard, apparently. He could not help but smile.

"That's better. But you have a brother and I had a sister," Emily offered with quiet certainty, nodding, slowly looking up to find him. "I was very young. She was younger, just a baby, just this high...." Emily held up two fingers in a close pinch and peered through them with a half-closed eye. There was nothing funny or lighthearted about the memory of her sister, Patrick could see.

"Now that is something you have not told me before," he said. Emily had no sister that he knew of; he would have to check.

Emily began to drift. "*Alessandra Elizabetta Marsh,*" she said, naming Alessandra completely. Shifting back, she said, "I imagine your home in the desert, Patrick; how it must have been, the love there."

"Yes, yes...."

Her eyes opened wide and she pointed. "See...? Look!"

Patrick turned. There was no one there.

Emily suddenly laughed aloud. She called out. "I wish you boys had a sister! She'd be pretty and happy. I'd give her dancing lessons and she'd wear a flower-patterned dress!"

She continued with her one-person act. "Like the one you're wearing?" she asked, her voice shifting.

"Yes, just like this one, only smaller: prettier, too; made of cotton with patterns of golden poppy and peony; tied about her waist with a bow!" She laughed. "Her blonde hair would be pulled back behind her ears and tied in place with a barrette."

"What's a barrette?"

"It's a clip that holds your hair in place; hers would be made up of diamonds... not real diamonds, they would just look like diamonds!"

Emily closed her eyes again. Patrick called after her. Her eyes flickered opened and then found him. "Did you see her?" she asked.

"Who would that be?"

"Alessandra."

"No, I'm sorry, I didn't."

Emily fell at last. Her eyes closed, and she slept, her breathing quickly becoming deep and regular. Patrick waited a moment then leaned across the bed and kissed her. He kissed her forehead, then lightly on her mouth. Her eyes opened.

"Why did you do that?"

"I don't know. It just felt right."

Emily again closed her eyes, puzzled and pleased. "Good night, then, Doctor Marsh."

"Good night, Emily."

DANAKIL

Patrick understands Ethiopia. He had lived the greater part of his life under the Ethiopian sun. But what Patrick knew about Ethiopia, he had learned from his brother, not because Bekele had given instruction or had lectured on the geographic or socio-politics of the region, but because Bekele was Ethiopia; at least, the heart and soul of what Patrick thought of as Ethiopia.

They had been walking for half a day following the dry gravel bed of the Awash River as it twisted and turned across the featureless landscape. The relentless, encompassing, suffocating heat surged up from the gravel, rushed past them as if from a kiln, desiccating their exposed flesh so that it felt more like sun-cracked canvas instead of their own skin.

Patrick called after Bekele who was a good hundred meters ahead of him. "We will die here! Are you happy now?"

The flow of hot air was upward but the force downward, numerically adding to the far more focused pressure of the swollen blister of the sun. Bekele turned, silhouetted against the blinding glare. The heat didn't seem to bother him as much.

"Night is only a few hours away," he called back. "We still have lots of water and you have the gun. We will be okay."

"Then you won't mind if I hop on your back?"

Almost blind to all forms of sarcasm but knowing his brother, Bekele smiled, in the way Bekele smiled: hesitant, halfway there. "This is your journey as well as mine –

Francesco said so."

They stumbled across the lifeless rock and scrub beneath the glaring torch of the sun, and through the torturous, impossible heat, with each step, each reach of a foot, each jarring shock to the body, an agonizing ordeal in Patrick's memory. Thank God he had remembered suntan lotion. He followed his brother in mindless drudgery and pain, generously applying the lotion but with a desperate thirst and a strong desire to be standing in the garden in Addis Ababa beneath a light rain; or, better yet, immersed in a cool bath. He reached inward searching for the sensation of the imagined cool bathwater on his flesh but could not summon it. He'd rather be anywhere other than this desiccating hell.

Bekele looked back over his shoulder, past Patrick to the horizon. He'd walk for a few paces and then turn suddenly to check again, and then he'd resume.

"What's with that?"

"It is nothing."

"Do you think we're being followed?"

A nod of his head.

Patrick turned about to study the same jagged horizon. "How do you know?"

"I know."

Patrick glanced at his brother and then back to the horizon.

"Who?"

"They are Afar."

"...Are we in trouble?"

"Hard to say.... We have nothing they want. They must know that."

"Playing with us, then?"

"Maybe, or maybe not."

"Still not good."

"No."

Patrick had never seen Bekele like this: so sure of himself, so at home.

Bekele added, "You have the gun; get it ready."

Patrick shook his head. He had thought, as his father handed it to him saying, "For emergencies only," that there would never be an emergency so great that he would feel compelled to point it another human being, never mind pull the trigger. He did not say this to Bekele, but he was certain it was true. He could imagine no circumstance that might compel him to draw the weapon – to save Bekele, perhaps, but not himself.

Bekele noted his brother's reluctance. He turned about and started again along the loose gravel of the exposed riverbed but then long after Patrick's attention had drifted back to the intolerable heat, he called back over his shoulder, "You'd miss anyway," he said, drawing a smile.

"God, I like Bekele!"

"I'll introduce you to him someday."

"That would be nice."

"…You're not smiling," Patrick said.

"I don't want to; I'm done with smiling."

"You're impossible."

"Tell me about it."

They walked with the sun hovering in a white sky ahead of them, Patrick following a widening distance behind Bekele, the sun cutting through his clothing, turning him to cinder from the inside out. Occasionally, like Bekele, he'd glance back over his shoulder; once he imagined he saw a dark form duck behind a boulder: an illusion perhaps, caused by the heat. But if not, whoever they were, they were close, less than a kilometer. A few more paces and Patrick stopped in his tracks. Turning about, facing the way they had come, he carefully and conspicuously withdrew the revolver from his belt, lifted it high over his head, then carefully and ceremoniously placed it onto the sun-scorched gravel of the ancient riverbed. Bekele, who had turned when he heard his brother's footsteps cease, nodded his understanding. "Okay...." He glanced at the horizon and back to his brother and added, "That's probably best." He then faced forward and continued onward as before, one foot carefully and deliberately placed before the other.

"That was a good idea. That was a really good idea to do that."

"I am a fool compared to my brother in situations like that, but I am not a complete fool."

The sun reached the zenith then slipped past on a slow descent. The heat felt just as oppressive but there was something for Patrick to look forward to now – the absence of the sun. The Afar would most certainly catch up to them but that hardly mattered unless the interminable heat could somehow be mitigated. In the absence of Hell there might be a chance; without a fried brain, a person could think.

Patrick saw how the present connects to the past in a box of old black and white photographs he had discovered in his father's study late one afternoon, the Afar carrying rifles and belts of ammunition, their women colorfully dressed but bent from laboring, and their children, gathered at their feet, staring quizzically into the camera. Like their ancient brethren, it was clear that the Afar belonged to the landscape. They lived and died within and upon that impossible sun-blasted desert, dark like the sand, poor like the rock, but unlike the tortured earth beneath their feet, fragile and ephemeral.

But the rumors of the Afar were not reassuring; they had been known to ambush Western tourists, those who would dare venture onto their lands, and hold them for ransom, even taking cash transfers from their credit cards for the so-called "Right of Passage" they offered. The Afar had also been known to raid the camps of the archeologists in the area, but that was rare because the Afar depended on those expeditions as a badly needed source of employment and income. But it was said that on one occasion, the Afar had ambushed an expedition's resupply van and held it and the passenger's ransom, the price of their release the tires on the truck. When the tires were off and stacked to the side, they promptly sold them back to the American scientists for all the cash and half the water in their possession. The important thing was no one died, that and the Afar presumably had a sense of humour so perhaps there was some hope after all, Patrick had reasoned at the time.

"I don't think it's funny, not one bit."

"I didn't think so at the time either."

"You and Bekele must have been scared shitless."

"I wouldn't phrase it exactly that way, but...yes, I would agree."

The light of day was changing; the edge of the sun-kissed earth casting shadows of sand-swept rock and ragged tufts of brittle grass against the cracked dirt. It was still blazingly hot. Patrick suggested they make camp. They had planned to sleep out under the open sky counting falling stars. Patrick won every challenge in their backyard in Addis Ababa. He claimed to see at least one a minute, exclaiming each time as one flashed overhead. "There!" with Bekele inevitably looking to the wrong sector of the sky without even catching a hint of the fading trail. "Missed it! Darn!"

"Again...?"

"Yes, again!"

"Next one, then."

"Right..."

"...There!"

"Missed it! Damn it!"

They would quietly laugh together.

Not tonight; tonight, he and Bekele would be sitting upright wrapped in their sleeping bags, their backs against a boulder, feeling the warmth slowly ebb while waiting for the first Afar to show themselves. It was as inevitable as the coming night that they would.

Patrick, having made his plans, waited for the right opportunity, and with Bekele preoccupied preparing their camp he slowly backed out, and then out of sight turned and ran. He sprinted then dropped to jog, jumping from boulder to boulder, following the ridgeline that fell precipitously to the riverbed. His hope was to draw off the Afar; they might even forget about Bekele who was dark like them, but a white man, so out of place, was something else again. A kilometer or so later, he stopped to take in his surroundings and catch his breath. He stood in the midst of a clearing ringed by sand-blasted boulders the size of houses. He slowly turned to take in his surroundings, still catching his breath. The stars were beginning to come out.

Motion: An Afar, and another to his right. Patrick slowly turned, knowing he was surrounded. He kept turning. Whoever jumped first, he'd be ready.

One of the Afar stepped forward from an unexpected direction. "I'm over here!"

Patrick jumped to face him.

The Afar addressed Patrick in Aramaic "Who are you?"

"Patrick Thomas Marsh."

"And the other?"

"The other?"

"We are not Fools."

"My brother – Bekele Amara Okello."

"...Thought so."

Before Patrick could reply, the band of Afar, men and women, children too, turned as one and disappeared, leaving Patrick singularly alone. He required a moment to realize what had happened, and then slowly backed, thinking to run for it, but immediately tripped over a dark object wrapped in cloth that one of the Afar must have placed directly behind him either to ensure he tripped over it, or more likely to ensure he didn't miss it. He climbed to his feet and picked it up. It was Francesco's revolver.

"Why did you run?"

Bekele. He stood in the clearing, his eyes shifting from the revolver back to Patrick.

Patrick held up the weapon. "They gave it back."

His brother slowly nodded. "What happened?"

They were suddenly interrupted by the appearance of a brilliant star in free fall. They watched it plunge in slow motion, and seemingly questioning the mathematical precision of its fate, held onto the ragged edges of the black hills for a few seconds before releasing its grip and slipping out of sight in pursuit of the sun, and in the process surrounding the day to the night. The sky fell into an infusion of gold, yellow, blue, and white; creation hesitated, waiting the length of time for a man to breathe before it suddenly unleashed a heavenly explosion: a cascade of diamond stars born within a momentary cataract of blinding light: heaven suddenly revealed.

"It is God talking to us," Emily said.

"It is God talking to us," Bekele said in wondrous awe, his head back. "We can only wonder."

"We can only wonder," Emily echoed.

"We will walk the *Danakil* together someday. Place our feet into the *Abhe Bad*," Patrick said quietly from beside her in his office overlooking the St Lawrence River.

Emily shook her head and said just as quietly in return, "No...."

"Yes, we will," Patrick gently pressed.

"No, we won't."

Patrick straightened; they had had this conversation a thousand times. "Why this, yes, no, yes, no?"

"No...."

"Emily.... Please."

Emily returned a sad smile, and would only offer, "Maybe," her smile slowly dropping off until it disappeared entirely. "With any luck."

The temperature was quickly dropping; it would be near freezing in a few hours. The stars were riotous. "Where does Heaven begin and the *Danakil* end, I wonder?" Bekele asked. He added, forcing Patrick to consider what he meant, "It was no small gift, brother, to witness such a thing."

"Can you answer Bekele now?" Emily asked. "You,

know: Where does Heaven begin and the *Danakil* desert end?"

"No, I cannot."

"Maybe you are not nearly as bright as you think, Doctor Marsh; ever think of that?"

"All the time."

"Good, keep it up then. And Bekele was right again," she added. "It was no small gift to witness what you did: Heaven suddenly unveiled.... You are so god-damned lucky, it drives me fucking crazy!"

Francesco picked them up a day later at the rendezvous. He helped them pack their gear into the back of the van. He turned on the air conditioner and handed each a special "rescue package" prepared by Alessandra. When he heard of what had transpired, he turned white. He placed his pistol in the glove compartment and locked it. He squeezed Patrick's shoulder as he reached for Bekele and hugged them both, saying only, "Don't tell your mother!" They drove home in silence for the countless hours it seemed to take before they found themselves once again safe in their garden.

With their dinner over and the abbreviated version of events relayed to Alessandra, Francesco left the boys alone. He did not join them as he normally would. Months later, he gave a clue as to why he hadn't joined them. "I could see that Bekele needed to say something to you," he said. "I could see there was something between you."

The heat, dryness, and unforgiving harshness of the *Danakil* were still with them as Patrick and Bekele sat on the stone steps leading into the garden of their home in Addis Ababa.

Bekele said, "I have decided to change my name."

Patrick wanted to argue but remained silent in the midst of his almost overwhelming fatigue. He had barely heard what he'd said.

"Bekele Amara Okello is the name I was given as a child. Someone I will never know gave me that name without knowing who I am. I want my name to say who I am, who I am today, right now. I want my name to say who I have become." Bekele turned to make certain his brother was listening. He took a deep breath and for the first time announced to the world the man he truly was and remains: "Bekele Francesco Alexander Patrick Okello.... For without you, I would be nothing; without you, I would not exist; without you, I would be dead."

"Bekele! God!" Emily exclaimed.

"He is my brother."

FIRST LOVE

Away from home but not away from the love that sustained him, Patrick stood alone on a sweeping hillside wrapped in meadow and crowned with woodlands, overlooking a valley of green and brown and gold, the wind rising, pushing against him. It was his last year of medical school just before his internship and he was thinking of love. Not the love of his life, not the real Emily – not yet. He was thinking of the woman he had seen that day, the day before, and the day before.

"My name is Patrick Thomas Marsh. I thought I might say something to you."

She looked up. One hand was centered on the page of the book she was reading, the other was taking notes on a yellow and lined pad. The ring on her finger was on her right hand. It looked like something her mother might have worn. She acknowledged him with a shrug of her shoulders.

"I saw you sitting by yourself here and I thought I would speak with you."

She appeared incredulous. "Why?"

Patrick sat down across from her. They were in the library next to a tall window opening to the college grounds. The light was pure and silver, falling on the table, illuminating the two of them.

"You had such perfect concentration; you were one with your subject," he said.

"And you thought to disturb me?"

She was completely matter of fact; there was no silliness in her. If anything, she was completely indifferent.

She sat back, folded her hands on the table, and waited for him to continue.

Patrick leaned forward.

"You are beautiful."

She simply absorbed the compliment, staring back at him.

Patrick lifted his hands and comprehending she did not believe it, he offered, "Beauty is a light in the heart."

She blushed at this.

She was thin with flawless, unblemished skin, and dark hair cut fashionably short. Her eyes were watchful, grey, clear, and curious. Her hands were delicate; Patrick watched her long fingers balance a pencil and spin it in place, carefully setting it down again on the pad. Apparently, no one had ever spoken to her like this; no one had been willing to risk the icy, almost acidic barrier with which she protected herself.

"Well...," she said, uncertain.

He could see she was struggling.

"What do you want?" she finally asked and more firmly.

"You are American."

She seemed surprised he could detect this as she nodded.

"Where do you come from in America?"

"I grew up in Boston and I'm studying at MIT. I'm in the UK for the summer and thought I'd take a summer course."

Patrick glanced at her notes. "...Harmonic series."

Now she was surprised. "You're a math major?"

"No, I'm studying medicine – final year for me. I'm so exhausted I walk in my sleep. This could be a dream. I could be dreaming you, and I probably am."

She laughed then. It was spontaneous and deep, and it transformed her.

What is love, Patrick wondered, looking up and watching pillows of cloud against the blue of the sky follow the wind along the length of the valley. Do I love this woman? Am I ready for love? He remembered how the last time he saw her she had turned back to her work, her eyes dropping to the text while the light from the window fell across the table about her. He had studied the movement of her eyes, watching them shift as they followed the text, marvelling at their beauty and depth, the purpose there, and the smile that lingered behind them. He was standing so close he could smell the soap she used.

"I'm dismissed?" he had asked quietly, nearly whispering.

She glanced up surprised he was still there and even more so that he had been watching her.

"See you later," she said blushing and then she was gone again, absorbed in her work.

Why her, Patrick wondered; of all the women he had met, talked to, worked with, danced with, why her? Somehow, she had slipped into his life, inexplicably, surreptitiously. Somehow, she had become every thought, every breath, part of every moment of every day. It was as if there were two of him, one that stood in the ward, felt the patient's brow, and answered the questions, the other obsessed by how the light fell across her arm and the way her hand lifted to brush her cheek.

Alessandra and Francesco visited for the spring break. With his father at work, he walked with Alessandra in the park. She was floating on air, bright scarf about her neck, coat open, her head thrown back to catch the sun, and her arm linked through his. The spring had just begun. The trees were full in bud. The branches no longer rattled. In the warming wind, they lifted and sighed.

Alessandra turned to him and stopped their progress along the path the first time he had mentioned her name – that's all it took; only mentioning her name: Joanna.

"Have you found love, Patrick; have you found love?" She laughed again and openly with the suggestion and hope of it, but not fully convinced he could see what she meant.

He had blushed; his normally tanned skin much lighter now that he'd been away for such a long while revealed the color change. "Alessandra, please!" he'd cried out but without denying it.

"You have! You have!" she cried out with laughter. "Tell me all about her, this Joanna!" She twisted toward him. "A mother always wants to know!" She laughed again, the sound, as always, carried golden and pure through the air.

He barely recalled Joanna now, and required a moment to recall her full name: Joanna Grimond – Joanna Anne Grimond. But what is in a name?

The gardens were in promise with a multitude of green shoots pushing up through the wet and black mulch, fragments of earth clinging to them still, the shifting and slowly transforming landscape betrayed here and there by a solitary yellow bloom, a secret singularity shivering in the coolness of the morning's light rain. There had been a planting perhaps the day before, but the roots of the fuchsias and petunias and marigold remained contained with no chance to take root, at least not yet.

Love is such a mystery, but he had loved her. He was certain. She talked about deep and personal things in her life such as the death of her parents, the sadness that gathered about her in the evenings and even in the light of day, turning away as she said this, glancing away and then back to him. Once she had seen him from a distance and, believing he had not spotted her, had gathered her books and quickly slipped through the double wooden doors without bothering to say hello. Another time she had searched him out in the crowd, asking where he was until she found him and, greeting him, kissed him on the cheek before settling in to stand next to him to talk away the rest of the evening. He loved her directness. He loved her passion for her work. He loved her clarity of mind. She told him once how as a child she often cried when hearing a sad country and western song, and he loved her for that. He loved the best in her. Of that, he was certain.

"You look very tired today," she had said.

"I stayed up all night. An old man was dying. It was certain he would not make it through the night. He was alone, so I stayed with him."

"That was very brave of you."

"He never regained consciousness. He just fell away."

"Why did you do it?"

"Because I will be a doctor and that is what I will do."

"...I don't think I could have done that."

"Yes, you could. You sat with your mother until she passed."

She had smiled sadly at that.

He imagined them lying in bed together, she, laughing into his shoulder. But that had not happened, not in that way; not in the way he had hoped for when he tried to imagine what love should be like. They had sex beneath the sheets in her dorm room, furtively, she, allowing him to take her in silence. She had seemed almost in pain with her eyes squeezed shut, her kisses returned through thinned lips. He loved her but in truth he had not so much as held her hand as they walked through the commons or kissed her beneath the waning moon like true lovers do. Sex on weekends – four o'clock in the afternoons on Saturdays. One might think that sex was everything, that it was at least enough, but it wasn't. Despite the sparseness of their relationship, he wanted to tell her how much he loved her, his only redeeming grace the fact he could not quite bring himself to.

"So, you are in love, then!" Alessandra laughed. She again stopped their progress along the path. "My little boy is in love! I knew you would find love eventually, Patrick. It is within you to do so."

Patrick squirmed. "Alessandra, a man...a son does not talk about these things. Private things...."

She reached across and touched his cheek. "Private things, yes; you need not talk about them." She placed a gloved hand over her heart to give her meaning. "You are such a warm man – and you know you should talk to me about this not so private thing – falling in love. It is something to celebrate. You should let the whole world know when you are in love – that is what the world wants. So, answer me this," and she waited until he looked at her. "Do you feel that you might be in love?"

"I feel many things."

"Because, if you do, then all I have hoped for you in this life will have come true; and, if it is true, all I can hope for is that love will stay with you. It is a great thing to be in love. It is even a greater thing to remain in love."

"Like you and Francesco?"

He had been calling Francesco "Francesco" for years at that point.

She smiled. "Yes, like your father and me." She let go of his arm, removed her gloves, and held his cold face in her warm hands. Keeping his face aimed at her as if she were about to kiss him hello or goodbye, she said, "My love for your father is the same, and not the same, as my love for you and Bekele. One day you will know what I mean."

Years earlier, in the early morning while eating breakfast, Alessandra poured him a glass of juice and surprised him by asking, "Why do you get up every morning, Patrick?"

Still half-asleep, he sipped the juice. He set the glass carefully on the table. "I'm sorry...?"

"Why do you get up every morning?"

"You wake me up, and I have to go to school."

She sat across from him in her robin-egg-blue nightgown, her hair pulled back and held in place by a purple, white, and orange flowered band of cloth. She smiled, settling her elbows on the table, dropping her chin into her hands. Bekele entered, threw back his juice and grabbed his bread and cheese then sat next to Patrick, pulling the bread apart and breaking the cheese.

"So?" she queried, acknowledging Bekele only with a lift of her eye.

Patrick imagined she wanted him to say something like, "The world is a wonderful place and I'm a part of it and if I stayed in bed, I would no longer be a part of it; I would miss everything."

Bekele looked from Alessandra to Patrick and, though

surprised by the ongoing conversation, remained silent. He broke off another piece of bread and shoved it in his mouth.

"You get up because you have hope and love in your life," Alessandra replied gently. "If you had neither of those, you wouldn't get out of bed, not ever."

"And if you do love this girl but it does not last, then I can only hope you will love again. It will be an even a greater love next time. I know this."

Love is such an odd thing. It is mysterious. It is both eternal and ephemeral. It can be expressed in so many ways, for so many reasons, with endless inferences and meanings; not just between a man and a woman, but between all men, and all women, nature, and God.

There was another memory, and, once again, it was a recollection of church and God, family, and the future. They sat in traditional order along the length of a polished pew in St Andrew's, ironically a Presbyterian church, one of the few in Rome. They sat in order: Francesco, then Alessandra, Bekele, and then Patrick, a short line of family. Francesco's long-time friend, a Canadian pastor, was to give the reading. He was the man who would one day suggest Patrick apply to King's College. "He is such a brilliant boy."

Patrick recognized the passage: Corinthians thirteen. The pastor read the verse in English and then in French, finally breaking into Italian, and as the holy words echoed in the close white of the church, Alessandra looked past Bekele to catch Patrick's eye. She had only smiled and then had turned quickly away but Patrick knew his mother well enough to know what she was saying: 'Listen to this.... Pay attention.... This is important.' He had nodded his understanding. Alessandra's smile shifted and then widened, and then again looking away, lifted her gloved hand and brushed back a strand of her hair, followed by gently, almost covertly, leaning into Francesco. Patrick noted how his father glanced in her direction; he noted how he secretly smiled, how he reached into his pocket and secretively handed her a folded tissue; how he let his hand touch and linger on Alessandra's, and how he let it fall away only to reach again for her hand. He noted how, back to paying attention to the sermon, she once again brushed back her hair with a quick flash of her hand while glancing at Francesco and renewing her smile. Patrick noted all these things, but it took him a while to understand what he saw there.

Later, years later, graduating at the head of his class from Sapienza, the honors pouring down on him and with his acceptance to King's College in his hand, Alessandra reminded him of that day. They were dressing for dinner and were later to attend mass at the Sant' Ivo alla Sapienza. The boys were to wear jackets and a tie. She helped him into his suit coat, and turning him and straightening his collar, she reached up to adjust his tie.

"Do you remember," she asked, letting her hands rest on his shoulders, "*Though I understand all mysteries, and all knowledge, have faith enough to move mountains, but have not love, I am nothing'?*"

He could feel her warm touch even to this day.

"It means a love of God as much as it means a love for each other," he explained with unintended impatience.

"Yes, that's right. You comprehend so much for such a young man. You are brilliant, but all your brilliance will amount to nothing and it will be a hollow talent unless you live to those words; in particular, the ability to love and be loved. And I don't mean just God," she added as she turned him toward the door and whispered up into his ear, patting his back, propelling him forward. "Go now."

Another time, another place. Years later. As clear to Patrick as just a moment ago, Alessandra saying, "I know your love for all of this, Patrick; I can see it in you. But, also, there is a darker side too, isn't there? With luck, that will fade as you understand more. We all speak to God in our own way."

"This?" he'd asked, trying to sound clever.

"This, this…. Everything surrounding us; the glorious between our birth and death."

"Take my hand?"

Joanna took it.

Fall: the leaves, riotous, golden, brown, and red. They walked together along the path through the forest, in step, their feet pushing through the fallen leaves flying up to float about them. The air crisp, fresh, smelling of the wet earth. The sun, though not warm, split into javelins of light through the raining canopy, eclipsing the falling leaves. Flashing free, crystalline and prismatic, the flashing sun temporarily blinded them, then was hidden, then was again flashing, as hand in hand they each in their own way glanced up to gather it in. The path followed a river, black and still, reflecting the dark overhanging branches against a colorless sky. The surface cloaked with colorful leaves hovering above the silent surface, held in suspension by some invisible force. Metaphors of their lives, Patrick thought long afterward: whispers cast upon the surface, lost, forgotten, and going nowhere, but nonetheless full of color.

Patrick pointed through the leafless black and brittle branches to the river. "Look where the river splits, left and right, as if it has hit a wall. To the right it flows into the lake; to the left, it meanders for miles through the country until it finds the sea."

She looked surprised he'd even mention it, and then shrugged, "Okay...," quickly looking over her shoulder at something else.

With Francesco returning from his meetings and after learning all there was to know from Alessandra, Francesco had turned to Patrick and asked, "So are you ready to introduce this mystery woman to us?"

"I'm sorry, no, not this time."

Days earlier, anticipating the moment, Patrick had asked her to join them for dinner, but she was busy.

"My parents have flown in for the weekend. They have come a long way. I would like you to meet them, if you are up to it."

She quickly made an excuse. "I don't think so.... I have an exam on Monday. I need the time to study. I'm locking myself away all weekend, I'm afraid." She smiled as she answered.

"Not even a quick dinner?"

"I'm sorry."

The meaning was clear, but Patrick persisted. "You don't want to take a chance with this, do you?"

"I don't know what you're talking about. I have to study, and that's all."

Patrick nodded his understanding, turning away so she would not see how he felt.

"What do you want from life?" he had asked Joanna at one point.

"I live for my work. My life is all about my work – you probably noticed."

"Is there no room for anything, or anyone else?"

"I don't know, we'll see. That kind of thing just happens; no one can predict it. What about you?"

"I don't know... happiness, I guess."

Later, he thought about it and realized he should have said just one word: contentment; "I wish to be content."

"Are you content?" he imagined Joanna asking in the light falling through the high window, even though he knew it was not a question she would ask.

"No, no.... Someday maybe." There was no contentment in the hollowness he often felt.

But in the present, speaking aloud in the quiet and solitude of the ward as he finished his late night rounds, again thinking of what he should have said while knowing that none of us is ever completely content, he added for Joanna's benefit, watching her look up in surprise as the words fell out of him, "I want to love and be loved just as deeply in return." He realized even as the words he chose bounced along the corridor he already possessed that gift, in Alessandra, Francesco, Bekele, and, of course, now Emily. Still, it didn't help, did it? Not entirely. They were all either somewhere else, gone, or going.

"What did you see in what's-her-name anyway?"

"Perhaps it was the way she sat by the window, the sun pouring down about her as she read; no more than that."

"I don't like her."

"Maybe I was a bit harsh. Joanna had some good qualities."

"I don't think so. She has nothing going on inside her.

Just work and more work. What kind of person is that? Not a nice person: a good person, maybe, but not a nice person. Now Alessandra, on the other hand...."

"Joanna was not an empty person; she felt a great deal."

"How do you know that?"

"We all do."

"I don't like her and that's it."

"But you've only heard my side of the story. Perhaps if you heard her side."

"She's a crazy, mixed-up, issue-driven, self-absorbed, cold-hearted bitch, that's what I say, and I don't know why you defend her!"

"Emily...."

"What?"

"Do I detect some jealousy? If so...."

"Ha! Jealous? Of you? Ha!"

At the airport to see them home, Patrick pushing the bags ahead of them, Alessandra said, "I'm sorry we were not able to meet your young lady friend, Patrick. She sounds like a serious girl."

Francesco was fumbling with the tickets and checking the passports. Patrick turned so he was speaking only to Alessandra.

"She's only a friend, and not even that."

"I know, dear."

"I don't really know her. I don't know who she is. She doesn't want me to know."

Alessandra smiled her understanding. She placed her hand on his arm. "Just ask yourself where she will take you, Patrick; if you can answer that, you will know everything there is to know. Where will she take you,

Patrick; where?"

Patrick remembered smiling at the simplicity of her advice, but also because of the truth he saw in it.

FRAGMENTS OF MEMORY

Patrick sat at his office window watching the snow fall. Big flakes slowly settling without a gust of wind: twenty centimetres, maybe more by morning. Coming down from the north; a low over Labrador. He'd stay over at the hospital tonight; there was no sense in risking the streets which would be plugged by traffic, nor suffocating on the trains overflowing with the thousands packed in close trying to make their way home. What would it matter anyway if he were home? There was nothing in his apartment. It was cold and sterile, more so even than the corridors of the hospital. Later, he might go up to maternity just to feel the excitement of new life; not like oncology and the lonely corridors just outside his office where there was often no future at all; life ebbing rather than flowing.

Patrick pushed away from the window, turning his back to it. He sat at his desk. Bekele had called earlier that morning, home now, safe and warm, his voice and his smile projected through the connection. He had called from the market, sitting at a table at Dembel Market, Addis Abba, the sound of English and Amharic and busy traffic in the background. "I'm home now. Wife good; my lovely daughter Isla – she says hi; they both do. Yes, it is good to be home. I hear you got twenty centimeters of snow yesterday."

"Don't rub it in."

He had called Alessandra immediately following and gave her Bekele's update – Bekele could only afford one call and the connection to the interior of British Columbia was often spotty. It was all good now; Bekele was home and safe; no more sailing the seven seas for him. He had, in addition, told her about the extraordinary sadness they all felt concerning Emily's father without bothering to elaborate; after all, what more was there to tell since Emily was herself walking along the aisle of death. Her extended fibrous-like tumor they studied day in and out, from every angle, cross-sectional data from the MRI, was inoperable, and any attempt to surgically remove it would surely kill her. They had to try something other than chemotherapy, which they already knew did not work and quickly, or she would most certainly die, likely within weeks. Those were the relevant facts; nothing else mattered. Why dwell on impossibilities? He spoke of all that and the fact he was hardly qualified to deal with Emily. He was merely the protégé, the brilliant young doctor from King's College who was only in Canada for a short while to learn what he could. Alessandra did not agree.

Patrick slipped out of his office into the empty third-floor hallway, ignoring the swirling snow outside, the sound of ice pellets tapping on the glass just above the sound of his footsteps. He swiped his way out of the ward, sprinted up the stairs to fifth floor, swiping in again. The halls were nearly deserted: only the duty nurses. They looked up as he entered and smiled. One, Nurse Kumbahaba, rested her head on her hands as if on a pillow, indicating Emily was resting peacefully.

He found Emily as the nurse had indicated, sleeping peacefully on her side. There was no reason Emily could not have remained at home; she was healthy enough, but he had insisted she be admitted and had signed the necessary paperwork, the attending physician not questioning, just looking up as he handed back the completed form, his eyes red from fatigue but saying, "That's okay by me. Where else can she go?" She had no one now. They both understood that.

Patrick sat in the chair next to her bed reaching for her hand. He had received a call earlier in the evening: double flash; red; emergency; Emily; a 911 call to the house where she lived with her father. The on-scene paramedics were being patched through. Run. He sprinted up two flights of stairs, listened to the paramedic, calm, matter of fact; gave advice, and when the connection ended walked down to Emergency to await her arrival. A few minutes later he took her up to the ward himself. The paramedics had found her on her kitchen floor unconscious. She had fainted, the emotional shock and exertion too much for her.

His mind adrift, exhaustion setting in, Emily sound asleep, he casually studied Emily's hand, turning it slowly over in his: her fingers, flexible, exquisite, carefully manicured, warm to the touch. He kissed her palm, then turned her hand over and kissed the back, and her fingers. He looked up to study her features: lovely face, delicate. She appeared perfectly healthy, if not a little pale; blonde hair in the style of the day, not especially short: pierced earrings – the same emerald earrings. He had not quite appreciated how much they suited her. He looked around for her barrette and could not find it. He would ask about it in the morning, make sure it was not lost. He sighed. He'd do anything just to allow her a few more months, weeks, even just a few days to just be herself.

"They are still my favorite – see?" Emily said showing him her earrings a week or two later. Patrick leaned in close to examine them and sat back. He nodded and then smiled. "They were my grandmother's. She said she wanted me to have them. They bounced right over my mother, and I got them. My mother was not too happy about that, I guess. Not that it matters; she is dead, too, you know; same disease as me." Emily tapped her head. "Runs in the family."

"They are lovely. They suit you," he said. "That and your barrette."

"Thank you! Different grandmother!" She smiled, tipping her head, as she reached up to verify it was still in place.

She mused, studying him. "I don't get it, though; why did you hold my hand and kiss my fingers like that?"

"Like what, and at what time?"

"You know.... And don't say you don't. I wasn't really asleep, you know."

"...Maybe I felt sorry for you; maybe that is all it was."

"Hmmm..." She smiled. "Okay, then."

"What's so funny?"

She suddenly leaned forward and kissed his cheek. "You!" she whispered; "You're the funny one, and a liar too!"

Emily stood in the doorway opening to his office. She was wearing an oversized knit sweater that fell past her knees, and an old pair of slippers. Her short hair brushed back: a touch of makeup and a faint smile.

"You're up."

Emily responded with a smile. "Of course, I'm up."

The medical assistant came bounding up from behind her beginning to apologize. Patrick dismissed her with a reassuring wave of his hand and she quietly retreated.

"You have quite a lineup waiting out there, Doctor Marsh," Emily said when they were alone. She leaned against the doorframe for support. She was still a little unsteady on her feet.

"So I do – and you recall my name: that's good," he said.

"It is on your door.... Are you always this busy?"

"Often.... Yes."

Emily indicated a leather couch against the wall, and not to the chair facing his desk where she normally would sit. "May I sit there? I might want to nap."

"You may. What happened to your intravenous? I didn't authorize its removal."

Emily sat facing him, sliding back against the cushions so she was comfortable, tucking her legs up. "I don't recall her name – the tall girl, dark hair; she's nice; she loaned me her sweater. I promised to give it back, but she doesn't want it back. I can throw it out if I want to, but I don't think I'm going to, I rather like it. It is a little big, though, isn't it? It doesn't fit, not really." She rolled back the sleeves and showed him her arm. The only marking was a bright red puncture mark. The sweater would be stained on the inner sleeve where the puncture would have bled. "Your permission was not required, Doctor Marsh, I'm afraid. I removed the damn thing myself. I hate those things. It hurts and doesn't do anything much except when I want to go to sleep, and then it is helpful."

Patrick indicated her feet. "What about the slippers? They are intriguing."

Emily glanced down at her feet. "Oh! Little bunny slippers.... Yes, of course." She looked up. "They were in the Lost and Found – the dark-haired girl, she's very pretty too, you know, said that she found them, but I don't know why the tongue is hanging out; it doesn't seem very bunny-like, does it? She didn't think so either. I wish I remembered her name. She's nice."

"You are probably referring to Janice; she is very capable, dark haired and tall, and, as you say, nice too."

"Oh, yes, Janice; I remember now: Janice, Janice, Janice: Dark-haired Janice who walks in beauty like the night."

He again indicated her slippers. "It's not a rabbit; I think it is a puppy."

Emily looked down and then laughed. "Oh!" She laughed again. "You're right!"

She is certainly animated, Patrick thought. "You're in fine shape this morning," he said with a smile, his first since Emily entered and since the morning began.

"I am! I most definitely am! I haven't felt so good in a long time." She pointed, and said, "I like that, I like that very much! You should smile more often. I am so glad I was able to assist you in that regard!" She glanced out the window. "Oh! Look, it snowed! And it is morning!" She unwound, stood, and stepped to the large window that took up half the wall, slipping past him. She studied the white-clad city, plumes of steam from the glass skyscrapers rising from the city core. Patrick had turned in his chair to follow her progress, glancing out the window to see what she was looking at. "And here I thought it was still summer!" She made her way back to the chair and sat, again facing him, smiling still, tipping her head and shrugging to indicate it was his turn.

"Do you feel any light-headedness?" he asked catching up.

"No, should I?"

He slowly shook his head. "Well, you seem a little... shall I say animated?"

"Oh, yes, those damn drugs that help me sleep and calm me down – we're just chemicals, aren't we? Change the soup and we are someone else." Their eyes locked. "It is nice to see you smile, Doctor Marsh," Emily said after a moment. "It really is. It must mean you like me," she added.

"I do like you." He had no idea he was smiling.

"A girl can tell. Do you know what they are saying about you: the nurses, and other female staff, including some of the doctors – the female doctors, I mean? I do ask them about you if they are female, and I know any woman would understand the question without filling in too much, or being offended, report me for being sexist, or some such thing. I can say you are quite the topic these days among the ladies." She hesitated, studying him as much as he was studying her, smiling when he did not. "You don't appear to be interested."

"Not especially."

"Confidence – they all say you have lots of confidence, and in your case rightly placed; not all doctors can claim that. Handsome comes up next, followed by brilliant, again, and, of course, intense. Women don't generally care how brilliant you may or may not be, but they all say that you are both very good looking and very intense. That and the fact almost all feel you are a bit of a dark horse, and you are, aren't you? The Indian doctor – I don't recall his name; I should, I know – says that kindness and brilliance are an unusual mix. That means you are also kind, I suppose. I think he means that, don't you?"

"You are referring to Doctor Ansari."

"Is that right? I really don't know him."

"You see him at least once a day."

"I do? Well, he says you're brilliant, too. He says you're going to pass, when I asked him if you would, and I did say I hoped you would. I didn't know you were still a student – What do they call that? Oh, yes, residency, right– But it is that dark horse thing that gets most people. Most, I should say many of us, don't quite know how to take you, and some are even afraid of you. Yes, that's true, don't look so surprised; you are so smart is why, and so intense; not everyone is as smart and as focused as you and it bothers people. But they are the chickenshits, the timid among us; the paranoid and the insecure. Those who are not afraid of you are madly in love with you! Like I am – I am in love with you. You also have an unusual accent, too, by the way. What is it?"

Patrick had tried to keep up with the varied descriptions but had failed: the variation he attributed to human nature and so did not bother to parse out the details. "It is just a mix up from speaking so many languages; I sometimes get them confused in my head," he explained evenly.

"The dark doctor – what did you say his name was again; it slipped right out of my mind again.... Never mind! – says you speak Hindi better than he does. How many languages do you speak by the way?"

"Seven, or so, fluently; a number more not so fluently. I inherited the gift from my father."

"What was his name?"

"Francesco."

"Is that an Italian name?"

Patrick stumbled over the question, offering neither yes or no.

"Do you speak Italian?" she asked.

"I do."

"You could speak Italian to me, you know; I speak Italian. I'm quite fluent. My father is Italian. My mother was English."

"I do, in fact, know you speak Italian."

Emily sat back, surprised. "You do? How do you know?"

"Your surname – Portinari," Patrick offered.

Emily continued to study him, her smile shifting slightly. "I missed something, didn't I?"

Patrick nodded without explaining.

"How much do you know that I don't?"

"Not nearly enough, I'm afraid."

She straightened. Her smile shifted. "So, I'm not okay, am I? Still not, I mean?"

Patrick was not yet prepared for what he knew he would have to say. "Has anyone spoken to you yet?" he asked. He was thinking of Emily's father; she didn't seem to know. "Dr. Ansari; the nurses, Janice or Anne; or Dr. Johnson from Psychology? You like her, I know; her name is Sharon: tall, long brown hair that falls down her back? You have talked with her for hours on end. She thinks you are very bright, and you are."

"What should they say? Is there something to say?"

"Do you recall anyone I'm referring to?"

Emily shrugged and smiled.

"Not Janice?"

"No, I'm sorry."

"The sweater you are wearing?"

She looked down along the length of the sweater. "Oh. Right." She looked up.

"Your slippers?"

"Puppies! Ha! I must be quite the sight!" She blushed and ran her hand through her hair, keeping her chin up.

"Do you remember how you got to the hospital?" Patrick asked carefully, sensing he should have brought the subject of her father up the moment Emily entered his office. He owed her, they all owed her, that much.

"What do you mean 'got here'? I've always been here," Emily said. She frowned. "Okay, I know that cannot be true – my father must have brought me in. Tests, you know: endless tests; it is the story of my life, you see. I imagine I'm waiting for the chemo to take effect." She pointed to her full head of hair. "See, I still have my hair!" She ran her fingers through it again before continuing. "You can't operate, that's what sucks. Still, it can't be too bad, can it?"

"How is that?"

She laughed. "I would be dead by now."

Patrick ignored her attempt to keep things light. "You have a widely distributed fibrous tumor probably initiated by encephalitis which you had when you were a teenager – you were seventeen. It is amorphous and has spread throughout the mid-section of your brain, notably the hippocampus, as well as the amygdala. Since it is so extended it is inoperable and, as has been shown, highly resistant to chemotherapy, at least what has been attempted so far – that was before my time, I know. Sounds bad, doesn't it, the way I say that, but it is not hopeless yet. We have a number of things we haven't tried – a focused beam of neutrons targeting only the microfilaments, for instance; I have some experience with that technology. There are a few experimental drug regimens we could try, too. I have a few ideas there as does—"

She interrupted him. "Oh, the rumored tumor…. I know all about that!"

"You have seen the irrefutable fact of it from MRI scans which we have shown you on numerous occasions, and we have talked endlessly about it – you and I and Dr. Ansari with both you and your father present."

"Oh yes, that's right. But you were not there, I know that much. But we have talked about all this before, haven't we? You don't have to keep repeating it as if I had somehow forgotten – and I do know I do forget things, but not that. I just don't feel it growing in me, I suppose, that's why I don't remember or think about the whole thing – the dying part, you know – too seriously. I feel quite normal, in fact, except for a few lapses in memory which you keep reminding me about, and which I cannot help, so please stop, it is getting annoying, and who cares anyway; I know you and you know me and I do know who I am; I feel like I'm me, so what is the big deal?"

"You have more than just a few lapses, I'm afraid."

"But I remember what I need to remember, don't I?"

Emily tossed her head back. "You know, I suddenly have the impression that I could be quite wrong, and you don't know who I am. You have not said my name since I came in. Why is that, Doctor Marsh? Are you testing me again? I'm getting sick of being tested: tests, tests, tests."

"Is that why you came in here, so I would tell you your name?" Patrick asked. "You could have asked Janice; she would have told you, or any of the nurses. You didn't have to come all the way down here to find out."

"Janice? You keep asking about her; I don't recall any Janice, and I don't know any of the secretaries – I didn't know you called them that, even. I thought they were assistants, or something."

Patrick considered. "You are Emily Martina Portinari. You were born in Montreal on 11 May 1990. You are twenty-seven. Your father's name was Edward, your mother's name is Robin. As far I know you do not have, or have had, a sister, but I'm still checking."

Emily frowned. "A sister? What the hell is that about? But Emily – I like that name. But I feel older than twenty-seven. That can't be right, but I'll take it for now." Her smile opened. "Usually it is the other way around, isn't it? You often feel younger than your years. Edward and Robin – I remember those names; they sound familiar."

"Do you know the name of the city you live in?" Patrick indicated to the field of skyscrapers, their glass fronts reflecting the river and the rolling snow-clad mountains in the distance.

"Don't you know?" Emily immediately shot back. "Do you not know where you are, Doctor Marsh? Please be precise!"

"And my first name, do you remember?" Patrick pressed, trying not to smile again.

"I'm not supposed to know that – you don't want me to look you up on Facebook, now, do you?"

"It starts with a 'P.'"

"Patrick."

"The city?"

"Somewhere in Quebec, La Belle Province. I know... give me a minute! Montreal!"

"That's right; very good."

Emily sat back, relieved. "See, I'm not totally gone!" She smiled and then snapped her fingers. "I remember now! You and I had a long chat, didn't we?" Her eyes opened wider as she remembered. "We talked about the horses," she added, amazed by her sudden recall. "It was in my journal!" She looked about. "Where is that darn thing?" She hit her forehead with the heel of her hand. "I have misplaced it, I'm afraid; just temporarily, I hope. Maybe you could help me find it later, if that is okay? And the Janaja...," she added. "I don't remember how to pronounce them; the Devils, you said – everyone died; it was horrible. You have some horrible stories – experiences. But you lived through that, didn't you?"

Patrick sat forward. "The Janjaweed?"

"Yes, that's them!"

He hesitated. "We didn't talk about that."

"But I remember it."

"Impossible."

"I can't imagine living through something like that. You are very brave, Doctor Marsh – Patrick, I should say. And no wonder you don't smile ever hardly. Life isn't always fun, is it? But I like your stories of Alessandra; the ice and snow, and I really do wish she was my mother." She sat back. "Ha! I can't believe I remember all that! Oh, and I think it was Alessandra who told me about the Janjaweed – or you did, I'm not entirely certain."

Patrick slowly nodded. He could not fathom what was happening within the folds of her mind.

"Alessandra – I know she's your mother, isn't she? She whispers to me sometimes. I hear her very clearly. She loves me, like I'm her daughter. That would make me your sister. Ha! By the way, Alessandra has the same accent, nearly the same, as you, in fact. That's strange for an English-speaking Canadian, isn't it? She told me just the other day that 'beauty is a light in the heart.' We were looking out the window together. Spring was just around the corner."

"Khalil Gibran."

"Oh, is that right? Ha! I know who that is! I remember!" Emily laughed again. "That's funny, isn't it!"

In some ways there seemed to be nothing wrong with Emily, but not this; this was something else.

"Kidding – I'm just kidding," Emily quickly said, her smile dropping as if she had detected his discomfort. "I knew Alessandra was quoting someone. But here is the odd thing; I could hear her quoting what's-his-name without words. Do you know what I mean? I mean, how can you hear someone speaking when there are no words spoken? Now that is weird, don't you think? You might be right; there very well might be something wrong with me." She laughed lightly. "Got your attention, don't I? I knew that would."

"This is not a joke, Emily." Patrick reached a sudden decision. He steeled himself. "I think it important that I talk with you about your father; someone should have days ago. I should have."

Emily straightened. She tossed her head back. "Oh, that."

"Do you remember that I met you when they brought you in and that we talked briefly?"

Emily slowly unwound herself from the couch and approached the desk. She had made her way back to the couch without him noticing. She leaned in. "I remember how you ran your hand through my hair, and you held my hand," she said slowly. "You told me everything was going to be all right." She leaned in further. She whispered. "I know you love me – or I know you are falling in love with me, which is pretty much the same thing, isn't it? I mean, it hasn't happened yet, but it will. Alessandra said so; she said, that the end is always there in the beginning, and that is true too, isn't it? It is with us, isn't it? So, if you go, if you think all of this is too much and you decide not to look after me anymore because you are afraid of what might happen between us, we will never know, will we?"

"Know what?"

"About how much we can love one another."

Patrick looked away, momentarily speechless as well as unnerved. He had not expected this, especially how it was all interwoven with Alessandra.

Emily leaned in further yet: nose to nose. "It's important."

"Why is that?"

She whispered as if it were a secret, "I don't know, but it is."

"How could it be?"

"Because I know I'm a goner otherwise – like my dad."

"God! I look like shit!"

"You were beautiful – more than you know. I noticed right away."

Emily tipped her head. "...I still have that sweater, you know?"

"You do?"

"Yep, and the slippers too." She tipped her head. "But I have often wondered: do I need you more than you need

me, or could it be the other way around?"
    "I'm not sure."
    "It is just a thought, don't think anything of it."
    "I won't."
    "Ha!" She pointed. "You're blushing! Ha! Gotcha!"

AWAKE

Emily sat by the window overlooking the city, contemplating the sky, turning from blue to transparent white. A pinpoint of light grazed the peak of the tallest building. She watched, waiting for it to move against the sky, thinking it might be an aircraft. It did not move. It was near dusk, the sky crimson and orange. Finally satisfied, she made her wish ... but could not finish. The words would not come; the thought could not be crystallized. She craved contact with another; she wished for warmth; she wanted to touch and be touched. Let her heart be touched and her body, too, giving her the physical proof that all of this was real, that she was real.

Emily collapsed onto her bed. She lay for a moment staring up at the ceiling then craned her neck to look out the window again. The star had disappeared, obfuscated by a low band of cloud: black, smothering darkness, a shroud over the distant city. If not for Alessandra, she would only imagine such things, only feel such things; she would not let the notion of death, nonexistence, consume her so. Alessandra changed everything. Without Alessandra, she would be nothing; she would be dead.

"Nothing lasts forever, no man, no woman, no monument – not the mountains, not the river, not our planet, not our sun," Alessandra had once said.

She often saw Alessandra encompassed by a golden glow, their mutual love flowing across the distance between them like a river. She wondered if Alessandra could see the river that flowed between them; she would have to jump across as she approached.

Alessandra sitting next to her in her cane-backed chair.

Emily realized where her mind was going; falling again, slipping into yet another world. She forced it to change direction. No silliness, no. There was no time for anything that was not tangibly real. She thought of the stars stretching over her father's cottage, an almost solid band across the sky, almost hurting her eyes in their brilliance. She imagined throwing herself off the end of the dock as she had done so many times as a child, or slipping without a splash into the lake, feeling the cool softness, surfacing, turning, floating on her back – looking upward, the starlight scintillating off the surface, infinity all around, enclosing her within a dark embrace.

It is a special, pristine place, she knew.

The light from the window caterwauled across the floor, over the foot of her bed, then disappeared into the corner turning the room dark and grey, black and bottomless. It would not be the first time Emily had considered the finality of that dark embrace. Her mind continually returned to that dark, deep, and protected place, that anchorage, that final sleep without dreams, that Undiscovered Country, as Patrick called death.

"Are you certain I'm not dead?" she had asked Alessandra.

"Do you feel dead, my love?"

Only Alessandra would listen to such nonsense.

"Yes – mostly."

"Do you want to be dead?"

"I...."

Emily shuddered. One night, falling into sleep, she would be taken, simply taken. Not alive, not dead, the end of all things, her dissolution and her antithesis, would climb up the outside trellis, force open the window then step silently across the uneven floor. The nightmare played and replayed as Emily slept, and even sometimes while awake, each time bringing waves of fear and nausea that spun the room and dropped her onto the bed. Death would come for her as she knew it ultimately would, turning her literally icy-cold throughout. "I am the deep thunder belching up from the sea, rolling across the land, pushing the inky blackness across the pinprick cold of the stars," Death would say as if rehearsing its lines before throwing her down into the tall grass and tearing her apart. Never satisfied, never consummated, its anger would tear her to pieces until there was nothing left. Not even Alessandra could stop it or mend the wounds inflicted.

"I... I feel empty and cold."

"Then I would say the answer to my question earlier is, 'No.' Dead is forever, and forever is a long, long time."

"But the next time I close my eyes I will be gone."

"You will be somewhere else; that is not the same as being gone."

"It is truly odd how the real sometimes mixes with the unreal, the reality of daylight indistinguishable from the shadows of night, where the *Danakil* ends, and Heaven begins," Emily thought. She wondered where the strange images in her mind came from. They were not her own. Was there anything, even her own thoughts that truly belonged to her? If not for Alessandra....

A hand grazed her shoulder and then returned, lingering for the briefest of moments before dropping away. She screamed but there was no sound. It stepped forward silhouetted against the window and reached for her. She laughed in staccato, "Ha! Ha! Ha! Ha! Ha!" Madness. Recovering, she screamed again, this time a real scream. A vast silence answered. The monster was white, it was black, it was a lost lover, and it was a killer. She was helpless, trapped within the four walls, ceiling and floor. She prepared to greet her final end. She lay back and threw her head back, exposing her neck, stretching out her arms. Only her nightgown would be between her and the end and she would have removed that if there had been time.

Death – for who else could it be? – stepped out of the shifting shadow and sat on the edge of the bed. The bed sagged with its weight as it drew back a loose strand of her hair and carefully placed it behind her ear. She opened her eyes, and with them open, she could see her destination now as clear as a bell sounding in winter; the verdant gardens on the far side of a dark river, the white-washed homes nestled along the shore, and higher on the bank, a woman wearing a light summer dress ruffled in the spring breeze.

Not Death but an angel – for who else would it be but an angel? —propped her on the pillow, carefully tucking the sheets about her. A handful of stars punctured the gray city sky. A cloud scudded past, picking up the light from the city below. Her room remained still. She waited for the angel to speak and she knew it would speak; she just had to wait for the honey of words to flow. There was a shift in the silence as the words it chose took a true form, visible even with her eyes tightly closed, golden and suspended before her. *"I have seen a diamond star chased by the blazing sun slip into the heart of the black desert,"* it said, and she knew then her angel was Patrick.

Emily intercepted his hand and placed it carefully on her breast then drew it along her body. She kissed him again, clinging to him, reluctantly letting him go only when he drew back. "You know I love you," she heard him say. "I cannot hide that fact. I am blessed, and cursed, and quite helpless in the face of how I feel."

She floated in the sea.

She opened her eyes.

Patrick held up a glass topped with water and ice. She reached for the straw with her mouth and luxuriated in the sensation of the cold water on her tongue. It was so cold; how did he manage to get it so cold? She emptied half the glass.

"There, now," Patrick said.

"There, now," she croaked back.

"You took a while to wake up."

"I didn't hear you come in."

He set the glass aside and helped her lay back. "Did I startle you?"

"You climbed into my bedroom through the window," Emily managed to say, brushing back tears, quickly turning aside so he wouldn't see them, wiping at them furiously. "You were standing in the shadow. You touched my hair...."

He gently turned her face back to him. "I saw you from the street," he said and nodded to the window seat and the cushions spread upon it. "Were you looking for me?"

"Yes – yes, I was."

He let his hand fall away.

Emily pushed herself upright, surprised by how strong she felt. The dizziness had all but gone. She felt wide-awake.

"I was making a wish."

"About what?"

"It's bad luck to tell."

Patrick sat back and studied her, then again smiled. He placed his hand on her forehead, keeping it there for a moment before letting it fall away. "No fever," he said.

"I thought for a moment you were going to kiss me," she said. "You kissed me before, remember?"

"I remember," he said.

"You can kiss me again, you know. I won't mind."

"Maybe later."

He reached into his jacket pocket. He had just come in from the outside, apparently. "Here, I have something for you. It is something I would like you to try. It will help, I hope." He twisted off the cap from a plastic container and spilled two out onto his open palm. Emily snatched them up and angrily tossed them away. They struck the far wall and clattered into the dark.

Patrick looked about briefly, then in the corners and on the floor then under the bed. He left her side momentarily to scoop them up, and returning he said, still smiling, "I guess I said the wrong thing."

She nodded. "You did."

"You should know these pills are experimental and very expensive." He added, "I would turn your room upside down to find them, but more important, to ensure you take them."

"I'm sorry but I like the way I am." She began to shake.

He drew her chin up, captured her eyes with his and waited until she calmed. Her barrette was hanging from a thread; he untangled it and placed it on the night table beside her, then kissed her forehead to settle her further.

"Who doesn't?" he said gently.

She eventually calmed, breathing slowly, leaning into him.

"I wish to tell you about my father," he said into the returning silence of the room. "It is important that I do."

"You have a father?"

"Francesco – I told you about him, remember?"

"He's not your real father."

"He is my father in every way."

"I always knew you had a father; you look like the type who would have a father."

"As do you. And that is something else I must explain; it, too, is important that I do. I am the responsible type, it seems. My mother is to blame."

"Okay," Emily agreed as she smiled, trying not to cry. "Go ahead. I like your stories."

"It is not a story," Patrick said. "I was interning at King's College. I was tired to my bones, the end of a twenty-four-hour shift. Alessandra called; the connection was as poor as usual. I had thought it might be about Bekele running off to sea – it is not the safest job in the world – but it was about Francesco. Alessandra said he was dead. Very suddenly. No warning. He hit his head, pretending he was young, as you might expect from a man who had such zest for life."

"That's very sad. Very sad, indeed. I feel sorry for you, Patrick. To lose a father like that when you loved him so much, and he loved you. My father is dead too – I found him sitting at his desk slumped over. I have never been so afraid."

Patrick sat back. "You remember now? I am amazed. I

did not think you did or could. Part of what I intended to discuss with you tonight was just that. I was prepared for the worst and not looking forward to it. I imagined talking about the death of my father would help you in both recalling as well as coming to terms with your father's death."

"Oh yes, I remember, so don't worry, and I do appreciate how you look after me like you do, Patrick, but it seems like yesterday, though it was a while ago that my father died, I know."

"It wasn't that long ago."

"How long?"

"A month."

"...Only a month?" Emily asked after a brief moment to think. She continued in a rush. "It seems longer." She sat up to explain. "I'm living in his home, you know. Of course, you know; we are sitting in my father's home right now, aren't we? Did I give you a key, by the way? Oh, I know I did! But you should know I never lived here as a girl; my father – his name was Francesco, too, you know. I bet you didn't know that. It is quite a coincidence, really, don't you think? He bought it after I moved out the first time. Before that we lived in another country, in Ethiopia. You wouldn't believe the gardens: blood-red hibiscus and curtains of purple clematis. I absolutely adore clematis, don't you, and morning glories too, they are especially nice? I live here by myself now. I have nowhere else to be or can go, really. It is this thing up here." Emily tapped her head.

"You have some help; someone comes by every day to make sure you're okay, get you something to eat, clean up, and so on."

Emily stared back, uncertain what to say.

"Why, don't you remember that?" Patrick asked.

"I know someone comes, a woman; I like her very much."

"Her name is Daniela. Daniela is from Syria."

"Is she old or young?"

"Middle aged – she has two children, Stephanie and Adnan. Her husband, Sayid, is a custodian at the hospital; that's how I came to know of her. I like her, too, and I did right from the start. She works hard and is quite trustworthy, as is her husband."

"I remember what you said when you took me upstairs to the ward," Emily said, switching, puzzled because she could not remember who Patrick was talking about. "You thought I was asleep or unconscious, but I wasn't. I recall everything you said, every word. You were quite upset. I felt sorry for you. I almost opened my eyes, but I didn't, did I?"

Patrick shook his head.

"You also said you were not about to let me go, not without a fight. But why is it a fight? I feel fine; just grand, really."

"So tell me again about your father," Emily insisted, lying back again with Patrick's help, all the while tracking him with her eyes. "Such as when the two of you stood in the desert and you hugged his shirt against your cheek, sand flying about you and Alessandra speaking for the first time: golden bells on silver threads, saying, 'We believe that with all our heart.' God, I love Alessandra! She has a real gift."

"So she does."

"There is no one like Alessandra in the world, is there?

I mean, there couldn't be anyone so perfect. We all suffer imperfections; most of us, that is. Look at me; look at you."

Patrick nodded again, expressionless.

Emily finally smiled, gaining her point. "You don't smile much, do you, nor do you ask what your imperfections are."

"They are too numerous to count."

"There is something in you. I worry. I know Alessandra does too. Are you afraid I am going to die?" Emily waited for Patrick to comment. She eventually said quietly, "Go ahead, then – tell me about them; both of them – not your imperfections; there are more than two, but you should know there is nothing big about any of them. Tell me about Alessandra and the man she loved. Something they did together. Something that demonstrated how much they loved one another so we can both take notes."

"I am amazed you continue to dwell so much on my mother."

"I need you to tell me. You and Alessandra and to a lesser extent Francesco and Bekele are all I have. Just tell me something, anything, please; you are so good at it."

"We should talk about you. I should insist we do."

"No, let's talk about you, please. It is a better story – I like it better. Mine is so boring.

"All right," Patrick agreed. "A short one and then we will talk about you – agreed?"

"Agreed."

"I was... ten, think. Alessandra grasped Francesco's hands and they began to dance with no music to accompany them other than what was in their minds. I remember Francesco crying out, 'Who is this crazy woman!' Then he laughed and drew her close, then lifted her so that only the very tips of her shoes touched the floor, leaning her back so far that she lay nearly on top of him. 'You have gone quite mad, my dear!' He laughed as Alessandra laughed, knocking aside the chairs and table, dishes off the counter, sending Bekele and I for cover. They danced and danced, and, finally exhausted, ended, breathless, turning to us and bowing."

Emily clapped as she laughed. "That's lovely, very lovely! I liked that very much!" She struggled to get up. "We should dance!" she cried.

"No, that would be ridiculous." He nonetheless helped her to her feet. She wrapped her arms around his neck, and they began to dance, slowly moving away from the bed into the wider room, Patrick's arms around her holding her close to keep her upright.

"I cannot dance without music," Patrick suggested quietly.

"Did they?" Emily challenged softly back, pressing her cheek against his. "They had no music other than what was in their hearts, as Alessandra would say." She turned with Patrick in the silence of the room, casting her head back, leaning back so that Patrick held her, turning with her again. She straightened and kissed him fully on his lips, her feet lifting off the floor. Back on her feet, she lay her head on his shoulder. "So, tell me again, Doctor Marsh, are we lovers?" She cast her head back to catch his expression. "Hmmm.... I think so, right? Maybe not of the body but in the mind?" She sighed and shook her head. "The body will come later, and not too long from now, I can tell." She smiled. "You should know that when the time comes, I shall not protest. I like you – I love you."

"It would be very wrong of me to do so; I am your

doctor and you are my patient."

Emily shrugged prettily. "Details, details...."

Patrick suddenly swept her up and carried her to the bed. He lay her down and then sat down next to her taking up her hands.

"Not yet?" she asked.

"Not yet."

"When yet?"

ABHE BAD

"So, tell me again, Doctor Marsh, what it was like when your father died? I mean, how did you feel? I mean, I don't feel much of anything, really, ever. I have nothing invested in the past; no love, no anger, no pity; I'm a broken record, a novel half read, and all that."

"What did it feel like when you discovered your father in his study?" Patrick asked.

"I felt nothing – nothing."

"That's not true, the shock dropped you to your knees. You managed to call 911 and then you passed out."

"The thing in my head did that."

"I don't think so." He switched and said, "This is what it felt like; from this you will know what it felt like."

Patrick stood on the shores of *Abhe Bad*. He stood within a desiccated and raw place, within a landscape unknown elsewhere, on an invisible line separating Ethiopia from Djibouti: fantastic but barren, grotesque but wonderful, impossible but real. He had been following the *Awash* along the same route he and Bekele had taken many years before, past the hills of *Afofili* where the ancient bones lay scattered on the sun-blasted surface, past the steep cliffs and molten pools of sulfur, and onto the open plain with its limestone chimneys. A band of indigenous Afar had been following him at a distance, but once his feet found the salt-blistered shoreline of *Abhe Bad*, they crouched behind the man-etched rocks and waited. This was home. This was also the end of it. There was nothing beyond, only empty time and place and the as-yet-unplumbed caverns of Patrick's heart, for after all his father was dead. Francesco was dead. Alessandra had said he was home now, back to the snow-capped mountains and green meadows leading down to the great river running slow before the village as if comprised of quicksilver. There was no need to revere his body, she had said, since we are not bodies. We are more than that.

There was rightness to where Patrick stood, a relevance he could not deny. With his lips blistered and bleeding, his skin cracked canvas, he fell to his knees and wept for his loss. His heart, his soul, was one with the landscape; he was the *Danakil*, the *Danakil* was he.

And yet, it was not silent where he knelt. The unrelenting wind hollowed the desert as if it was not quite real, and only the wind was real, and in that sound and in that place, he could hear Alessandra asking, "Why do you get up each morning?" and then answering for him: "You get up because you have hope and love in your life. If you had no hope you would not get out of bed, not ever."

"I have no hope, the same as my faith," he would answer her if he could as he wept. There is inevitability to our existence, Patrick would tell her, imagining her sitting back in her cane-backed chair. He would explain: life followed by death, love followed by loss, existence to oblivion, a one-way path, a collation of random events we try to understand and attribute meaning. It is the pattern of our short lives, he would say. In the end, there is no reason to get up, none at all. We are dead before we are born.

Patrick shook his head and tried to concentrate. This is but another dream; none of this is happening or has happened. He did not really stand in the midst of the *Danakil* near death. Alessandra was just a figment of his imagination, Francesco too, and Bekele; his bed at night, the gentle lifting of the curtains. Our lives are mere delusions, mysteries that we build within ourselves. This is where the *Danakil* ends, and the dreams begin, he finally knew as he fell forward onto the hot griddle of rock and sand. He struggled back onto his knees one last time his hand burning on the hot rock, and collapsed again. This is it; this is the end, he thought.

Patrick turned onto his back to face the silhouette of what could only be an angel hovering against the blinding sky, floating, feet off the ground, its wings spread. He struggled to his feet, his heart racing, almost flying out of his chest; he would be on his feet when he met his maker. He didn't make it; he fell forward again, with only enough strength to roll onto his back and look upward to face his destiny with his eyes open.

The silhouette drifted downward and, landing, placed its feet on the desert floor, folding its wings. A white sheet flew over him like the wings of a great bird, fluttering, settling over him. A gush of water filled his mouth, and another. A wet cloth was placed on his forehead. A woman's hand opened the collar of his shirt and salved his face and lips. He knew it to be a woman; he could hear her singing deep within herself, the sound low and rising and aimed directly at him, that and her touch made the fact she was a woman indisputable. She poured a dribble of water over him, keeping her hand on his chest to check the beating of his heart, saying as she looked up into the sun, "He will live."

Not Alessandra; it was not the sound of her voice.

"We have been following you since *Afofili* and many days since," the silhouette said from out of the glare of the sun. "Have you completed your journey now or is there more? Do you want us to let you die?"

Patrick opened his mouth to answer. Nothing came out. He shook his head.

The woman – a woman's eyes above the burka – poured a trickle of water into his mouth, letting an excess splash against his face. He closed his eyes in the sense of relief it gave.

"I have seen you about the market in Addis Abba," the silhouette added as it hovered over him. "Your white mother and father, and you and your black brother. If you are that white boy, I hear you speak all known languages. It is quite a gift. They sent you away to school to learn medicine."

Patrick nodded.

The silhouette knelt next to him and continued, shifting to Aramaic from his native Afar. "So it is you. The first time, years ago now, you and your brother walked this same path. Your brother's reason for doing so I understood; your reasons I was not so sure of until I realized you were brothers. I am not likely to forget, even if you have."

Patrick attempted to sit up but was pushed back with a gentle hand on his chest. The woman again.

"So, it is you then," the silhouette asked, reaching for a response.

Patrick nodded; the world was spinning; he could barely breathe.

"God spoke to us, then," the Afar added from what seemed miles and miles away.

Patrick, remembering, arched his back and cried out, "Oh, God!"

"I decided then to let you and your brother complete your journey. We did not interfere, although we followed you for many miles as we did this time, but only you. So why do you walk now? Does your brother still live?"

Patrick nodded, racked with pain, pain for how he inwardly felt as much as the pain he felt in his body.

"Who has died then? Why else walk the *Danakil* and cut one's face like that?"

"Our father," Patrick managed, his voice breaking.

"What was his name?"

"Francesco Alfonso Tosselli."

"Ah.... I heard he died. I liked him well enough. Your father was no more Italian than I am, but he loved us all." The Afar was sitting close, beneath the shade of the sheet that flapped in the desert, his hand now resting on Patrick's shoulder. "When you are better in a day or two, we will take you home," he said.

"Home?"

"Where else would we take you?"

Patrick floated upon a shoreless sea with an open sky above and endless depths beneath. He could not feel his body; as far as he knew, he did not have a body. He opened his eyes to catch the sudden smile of the woman hovering over him; her smile was in her eyes. The world is beautiful, wondrous and sad; it is all so mysterious, Patrick knew at that moment as he slipped into unconsciousness.

"Of course, it was Alessandra! Did you ever have any doubt?" Emily insisted later. "She sent the Afar to find you, the first time to make sure you and Bekele were safe, and then the second time to rescue you from – what was that, a suicide attempt? Tell me it wasn't! Tell me that it was! Tell me the truth!"

She suddenly leaned forward and ran the tips of her fingers across his cheek.

"What's this?"

"A scar."

"Did you do this?" She leaned in closer to see, her fingers lingering on the scar. "I think you did. The Afar would not. He was rescuing you. Alessandra sent him. Isn't that right?"

He would not answer.

"And what did Alessandra say, and your brother?"

"Bekele threatened to kill me – save me the trouble next time."

"I thought so. I would too." She slapped his arm hard, once, twice. "I should beat the shit out of you!"

She calmed and sat back controlling her breathing. "The three of you held a memorial for Francesco, I suppose?" she asked.

"We did; over three hundred people attended. The hall overflowed. Attendees included the entire Italian consulate, friends, neighbours, at least a hundred that knew Alessandra through her work with the Canadian Red Cross. Local people who knew Francesco even just a little gathered in the parking lot, sitting in the garden drinking their tea, and *tella* which is a widely available alcoholic beverage in the area. We held his memorial during the day when most had to work, but still they came. It was very moving. I had no idea he was so loved by so many until then."

"Why wouldn't you? You loved him; Bekele and Alessandra, too; the Afar. Again, I cannot imagine what Alessandra must have felt."

"Should I have a memorial for my father, I wonder?"

she asked flatly when Patrick did not respond. She was still fighting with her anger.

"It is up to you."

"Would you come?"

"Of course."

"I am somewhat tempted because I could take note of who came and then see if I could remember them."

"There is that."

"Remind me tomorrow, okay?"

"Okay."

"Or I could write it down on my foot, I suppose. I have lost my journal, you see. I will never remember if you don't."

Patrick smiled.

Emily's slowly returning smile opened in response, her anger dissipating. "That's better...." She nodded catching his eye, nodding. "Better."

The nurse came and went and was gone for an eternity before returning. "You had a visitor. She said she was your mother, although she looked too young to be your mother."

"Alessandra."

"Yes, Alessandra. She has quite the presence. She left you a note." She handed him a piece of white paper: the old kind, heavy to hold, rich in texture. It was cut to length and then folded in half.

Patrick, love, I suspect you now know where the Danakil ends and, more important, what lies beyond. See you tonight. I will tell you a story, one of your favourites to help you sleep. Help you think of snow, swimming in a river, or maybe light rain on a cool evening. Ha!

Love, Alessandra

P.S.: Thank God you are okay – I never would have forgiven you otherwise. Just sayin....
    A.

EMILY HAS A SISTER

Emily turned slowly about to look out the window. No hint of dawn. The night full. She grasped the sill searching out the shadowed places, light and dark, then returned to her bed sitting on the edge. A photo album lay on her nightstand. She reached for it and then opened it at random. She would go through it one more time without Patrick. She would do this on her own.

It had been a long time ago and meant almost nothing now, but Emily had had a sister once. It was not a dream. It was real. Patrick had told her it was true and not another world, another dream or false memory. How can my memories be false; did I not live them? Why would I construct something that didn't happen to me? She reached beneath the coverlet and could still feel the lingering warmth of his presence. It had been real then – he had been with her.

"Please look through this photo album I found in your father's study downstairs," he had said. "It will help you remember."

"That and the drugs you give me. I have to take a hundred or more a day, it seems. I hate taking them; by the time I reach ten I gag. One day I'm going to puke them all up, and then what you going to say!"

"Yes, there is that – but not a hundred, not even close; just twelve. Keep with it, though; they are beginning to help you, I can tell."

"How is that?"

"We would not be having this conversation, like this, if it were not at least somewhat true."

"Perhaps I don't want to remember, ever think of that?"

He offered the album to her again. "Look at that photograph; do you recognize anyone in it?"

"I think so – but I don't want to look. Please don't make me look."

"Who?"

"...My father. ...My sister.... My mother, I think."

"You had a sister, Emily."

"...I guess so."

Patrick had gone back to work; how he could find the time to look after her as much as he did was a gift. "I seem to have no free time these days," he had said, "but if this is what I have to do, that is come to you rather than you come to me, then that is what we will do."

"You know that's a lie," she'd thrown back at him, knowing as well as he the real reason; she was the real reason. He loved her; he just would not and could not say, not outside her dreams, the dreams that came and went, forgotten and then remembered.

The night before they had talked, talked, and talked. He was lying next to her in her bed, she listening to his voice through his chest, his steady breathing, and the rhythmic beating of his heart.

"How close can two be other than body to body?" she had whispered, snuggling closer.

"We are not our bodies," he had quickly replied, without weighing his response, she could tell. It was her favorite tactic – say something out of the blue, and then see what happens.

"Ha! That's Alessandra speaking!" she had said. Sometimes it worked, sometimes it didn't; that time it had worked.

The room - empty now, Patrick somewhere, somewhere - slipped away as the world of her past slowly became tangible, possibly real - but only possibly real because it was often difficult for her to differentiate truth from what faded in and out of her mind. The photos which were obviously a true thing - you could measure them, weigh them, put them away and bring them back out when you felt like it. She could rely on those, she supposed; exchange the not so tangible for the tangible.

She attempted to lift the images of that time out of her memory, embracing all she could recall tightly about her, fearing them, and yet needing them, and on the pages of the photo album before her it was spring. Emily, her father, her mother and her sister - that must be who they are: man, woman, a child of ten who must be her, and then a baby perhaps only a year old - had once stood upon a hill that stretched into a field of yellow and green with a dark river running through it. The river flowed dark and quick as the meadow topped with a sea of blood-red poppies swaying back and forth. Emily could once again feel the summer wind wrap about her; warm and safe, she again watched it slip up the slope, glide toward her, and then feel it flow past, gently lifting her hair and the fabric of her dress. Another gust! Ha! The sister of the wind before running up the hill! Emily could both hear and feel, even see, the low and hollow sound of it like soft breath, like someone breathing. The breeze pushed the gold and red before it, the colored heads drooping, straightening, carrying through, nodding back and forth, back and forth before finally settling to lean once again toward the sun. Emily spread her arms and wondered what it would be like to fly; catching an updraft until she was an almost invisible pinpoint against the fathomless blue sky.

They ran together, father and daughter, the rows of poppies snapping by. She tripped over her feet and was down with a laugh, rolling: the sky and field, the sky and field, then scooped up – and life became, once again, the moment the bullet pierces the glass, the moment the humming birds' wings can be seen, the moment a drop of rain impacts the smooth waxy-green surface of a leaf then slips, broken and splashing onto the dark surface of the pond.

Time, unfettered, landed her back in her father's reaching arms. The figure before her appeared so much younger than the man she remembered. But, of course, he must have been only five or six years older than she was at this very moment. Had she ever remembered how long his hair had been, how tanned he'd been or as strong, or even as affectionate? Her immediate memories, such as they were, and fading in and out too, included a man who was burdened with a deep sadness and was often distant.

What was her father's name again? What was his damned name? Patrick would know; she would insist that he tell her, and next time she would not forget. But how peculiar memory is, how selective, how quickly misplaced until the right circumstance, suggestion, perhaps the right chemical balance in the brain – thanks to those damned drugs in her case, and the photo album of course – prompts memory to unfold its wings to present a world that could have happened only yesterday, or a lifetime ago, or not at all.

But none of this may be real, she thought. It probably wasn't; it was probably just another hallucination. What to do? What to do? She turned her head and looked, and followed the long arrow of her father's arm to a time and place that existed within the complex network of her memory, beneath a canopy of chestnut, elm, and maple, as well as the shine of the newly unfolded leaves as bright as the green of the grass upon which her mother and sister sat. "Ha! Ha! I see! I see!" Fragments of light stabbed through the spinning leaves of the willows, and, in the background, the curve of the river as it swept out of sight behind a curtain of cattails, their dark ends nodding in the sun. Emily shifted to the image of her mother: the same color of hair and a face not dissimilar to her own. A woman's face, a content face, and a happy face.

They sat on a red-and-white-checkered blanket, the wicker basket open, the contents spread out. Red, green, blue plastic glasses: "One for me, one for you, one for me one for you." Her mother poured each of them a glass of pink lemonade, a thin arm white as snow, like Emily's; long fingers, carefully manicured, painted bright red. Look up, look up... now turn your head: her sister; yes, her infant sister, rooting through the contents of the basket and about to pitch forward into it: same color of hair as her mother, similar to Emily's except it floated about the child's face, sifting morning sunlight lighter than an air. A child, a beautiful child.

She tried again to recall her mother's voice.... It was almost there, almost real. "Here you go...." Ha! She remembered that, even with the sun placing her mother in silhouette, her features unseen. Something else, something else... Oh yes! Her mother folding back the wax paper to reveal a completely crushed sandwich – not that that mattered at all; peanut butter and honey sandwiches can be crushed and still taste as good. But she remembered the taste: the sun-warmed texture, the softness. It tasted wet; it was wet – a jar of slender dills had fallen over and soaked a corner. She took a bite and the all-encompassing taste of peanut butter and honey with a hint of dill, the peanut butter sticking to the roof of her mouth, came flooding back. She reached for the lemonade, aiming the plastic glass to her mouth, and missed. A trickle sliding down her chin. She caught it with the heel of her hand.

In the midst of that warm day in June with a day so perfect the absence of it hurt still, her mother unexpectedly handed over her sister, lifting her up, arcing her through the blue sky and sunshine, and setting her down next to her. "Hold your sister for a while, will you Emily?" she remembered her saying – she had a lovely voice; very sweet, ringing true now: "I'm going for a stroll along the river," she added, climbing to her feet. And then a man's voice – her father or not her father, who could know – distant beneath his hat, asking, addressing his wife, "Do want me to come along?" He had been there all along, bemused and content; Emily could feel his contentment; it was in the way he lay back on the checkered blanket with his straw hat pulled low.

Memory captured forever by the camera, but all Emily could recall from that point forward was that, filled with the sandwich and lemonade, and overcome with fresh air, she could not keep her eyes open. She and her sister – Emily could not quite recall her name but was pretty sure it began with an E – proceeded to sleep the sleep of angels beneath the summer sun, the breeze having dropped, the river dark and deep flowing along its bank.

"Thank you for helping me remember."

"I expect more will come with time and the right trigger."

"How? If I am so broken, my brain filled with fibrous micro-tumors, or whatever it is spread all through my brain so you cannot operate, how? Chemo does nothing; we have proven that; I damn near died from that. Maybe I should have. Next time you decide to take a stroll through the *Danakil*, let me know and I will accompany you!"

Emily sighed her frustration, shrugging it off. She pointed to the album. "What is her name? Is it written in here somewhere, on the back of one of the photos?" She was pointing to the little girl who she believed was her sister sitting next to the attractive woman she believed was her mother who, in turn, was sitting next to another little girl who Emily had been told was herself at age ten.

Patrick recovered the album and set it aside. She could see that something was not right.

"What's wrong?" Thinking she knew, she leaned in close. "Oh, I didn't mean that," she said softly. "I didn't mean to say, 'The next time'.... It was wrong of me to say that. I know because...."

He placed a finger across her lips. "No, it is not that; there is something else."

Her heart fell out of her. She braced for the worst. "Such as?"

DRUG INDUCED

In another fragment of memory, also true Patrick had told her, carefully turning her face up to his so that she could see the truth he spoke, Emily had once sat in her father's study settled back in a plush leather chair.

"You asked your father about your sister," Patrick reminded her, determined to break open her memories, so he had said.

"I have a sister?" Emily had again forgotten. She hesitated then asked, "What did you give me? I feel this nervous twitch in my stomach, and I feel like I am flying. You gave me something, some drug. You know I don't like that."

"It is a drug, a drug to help you remember; an acetylcholinesterase inhibitor, normally given in small dosages but we're prepared to up the dose in an experiment. I'm hoping to stabilize your memories so that once you remember something you will not forget. You will have to trust me, and Dr. Ansari too; we know what we are doing."

"I don't want any of your drugs. I like the way I am."

"We talked about it; you agreed."

"I'm not sure I should have."

"What do you like about not remembering your past? The past is important."

"Not as important as the present," Emily stated with an edge. She waited and then said, "You are my present; you are what is important: you and Alessandra. You are also my future. Please do not tell me if you think that is not true; I don't want to know if it isn't."

Patrick leaned in close. "Of course, it is true; you know it is." He straightened and smiled down at her.

"I'm not as crazy as you think, you know," Emily said, "and you are making me mad right now. I'm not stupid, either." She began to cry, the drug beginning to have an effect. "But why aren't you holding my hand? You are supposed to holding my hand!"

Patrick lifted Emily's hand to show their fingers entwined. He leaned in again, and again whispered, "I'm not about to let you go, not now, not ever. This will not take long."

She turned her face away and continued to weep, her eyes welling over.

Patrick called after her, "Okay?"

"Okay," Emily agreed, nodding without turning back.

Patrick glanced back over his shoulder. "Dr. Ansari is here – he's my boss, so see if you can behave yourself this one time; will you, for me?"

Emily turned back, her eyes finding him and not leaving him. She nodded and tried to smile.

"And there is an anesthesiologist here who is helping me administer the drug – Dr. Langley; I don't think you have met him before. And then there is Nurse Kumbahaba; you know her; you said you liked her, and I know she likes you."

Emily's eyes remained locked on Patrick. They didn't shift. "She is black like your brother Bekele," she said.

Patrick nodded. "Yes, that's right."

"You are right, I like her; she is very kind – she has kind eyes," Emily said, her eyes still locked on him.

Patrick glanced at the nurse and smiled then turned back to Emily. "Are you ready?"

Emily nodded.

"Squeeze my hand."

Emily squeezed Patrick's hand.

"We are going to slowly increase the dosage. You will feel a slight tingling sensation and might be feeling a bit disoriented, even dizzy. You will tell me if you feel too dizzy, won't you? You might feel a little nausea."

Emily gasped as the drug hit her.

"This is about your father, Emily. His name was Edward, not Ed, or Eddie – he preferred Edward, didn't he?" Patrick asked gently from what seemed a long distance away.

Emily nodded briskly. She was swooping downward then rising to clear the dark water – dark and deep and pristine; you can see the bottom twenty feet down.

"Are you still with me, Emily?"

"Yes, I think so."

"What's my name?"

"Patrick," she whispered.

"Okay…. Now, as we up the dosage, imagine your father; think about him, imagine him. Do you see him in the corner by the window, turning slowly toward you? A good-looking man, and well dressed. You look like you would be his daughter."

"Yes."

"Ask him about Elizabetta, or anything else you might want to ask him. Just talk with him. He wants to talk. That is why he asked you to come to his study, to talk. He has something to say, and so do you."

Emily turned her head on the pillow to where her father stood across the room from her. "Why didn't you tell me I had a sister?" she asked him. She swung back to

Patrick. "I had a sister! I remember! I'm not that gone, there are a few pieces left!"

"You need to address your father, not me," Patrick suggested gently.

Emily recalled only fragments of what she needed to know. "Why didn't you tell me I had a sister?" she asked her father, Eddie, Ed, Edward.

Her father, deceased now, two years gone at least as far as Emily could remember, flipped through the pages of the same photo album she and Patrick had studied earlier together. He barely acknowledged her presence. She knew that was a lie; her father had felt everything; there had been no stone in him, nothing cold. He had left her on a cold day. He had left her with his heart broken, not brave enough to face the future. Sometime between then and now, Emily remembered her father crying. He had stood facing the wall, his forehead pressed against it, his hands placed as if holding it up, his body shaking.

"Papa?"

He didn't turn. He slowly pounded his forehead against the wall.

"Papa!"

Then he turned. She had not recognized him. It was a man who resembled her father but who had eyes that were not her father's eyes.

Somewhere in the photo album there was a photograph, in faded color, curled around the edges, showing Emily as a child: pink dress, tight curls, her head thrown back, and a smile on her face that declared for any who dared to question, the world was hers. She hadn't seen that one; she wondered how she had missed it. Behind her towered tall cypress and, farther still, fields of green and gold dipping to the horizon. She was holding a much younger child's hand – her sister's hand, this possibly the first time Elizabetta had stood upright, albeit with support. Her mother stood behind, a hand on each child's shoulder, revealing long, slender fingers, a wedding ring, and an emerald glinting in the silver sun.

She held that photograph now in her hand. Patrick must have handed it to her.

"I like her ring," she said to the wider hospital room. "I wonder what happened to it. She must have hidden it away somewhere. Behind Herodotus? Is that where she left it? That is my father's favorite place to hide things like old photographs, letters, and money. I will check later."

No answer from anyone.

"Elizabetta looks like me, too, don't you think?" Emily asked, trying to gain anyone's attention. Where was Patrick?

Still no answer.

"It is funny how we live," Emily said, speaking to the photograph. "Our little souls here one moment gone the next. Elizabetta liked to laugh. She was curious, healthy; it was just that she couldn't breathe underwater. And my mother, she's very pretty; you never told me how pretty she was, Patrick. She must be nearly my age in this picture of her." Emily studied the photo more closely. "I'm not sure she's happy; her eyes aren't happy. Why is that, I wonder?"

Her memory suddenly unleashed. She gasped then said, speaking low and slowly, "I remember her by the river! You know the river? There is always a river, isn't there? I see her! My mother threw herself in, thrashing about, submerging, coming up, her hair in her eyes, and then on the shore, sitting, her knees drawn up, crying, and my father sitting next to her holding his head in his hands. Paramedics were there; first time I met them and many times since too, you know. I like them, most of them anyway; there are some assholes, as usual, though, aren't there? The fire department was there. Police. Flashing lights everywhere. A small crowd. Some of the women gathered crying, some of the men too. Kids like me. None of them joking around." Emily looked up searching for Patrick. "We all understand death, don't we?" she asked when she finally found him.

Patrick appeared frozen; for him time had stopped. Her father was now sitting at his desk, his eyes staring into the distance, a trickle of blood originating from his forehead meandering down his temple. The back of his head was blown away, plastered to the wall behind. "What happened to Elizabetta, Papa? What happened to me? What happened to you, and Mama?" she asked knowing he would and could not answer. Her father, nearly headless, climbed to his feet and went to the bookcase, and from the pages of Herodotus withdrew a folded note. He handed it to her, his eyes open but unseeing.

"I heard a bang and found him slumped over at his desk," she said, speaking to the room. "His brains on the wall behind him, blood pooling on his desk." She found Patrick and held his gaze. He had been unleashed by time and was reaching for her. "I called 911, you know, and then I fainted; the next thing I recall was you. You said everything would be okay, but it is not, though, is it?"

Emily buried her face in her hands but looked out a moment later to find herself sitting on the edge of the hospital bed in her nightgown, the one she brought from home. She wasn't about to put on those ridiculous outfits the hospital provided. It was part of the deal; she would not have agreed to all this otherwise. In the meantime, the IV remained in her arm and it hurt.

She tried to concentrate. Patrick stood beside her. The dark nurse had her hand on her shoulder. For a moment she imagined she might be Alessandra but, no, she wasn't. Another doctor to the side; Patrick's supervisor; dark-skinned. She couldn't recall his name, but he had kind eyes, those same kind eyes following Patrick, seemingly warning him, about what Emily couldn't guess. And still someone else out of sight behind her watching over the monitors.

"You are right, he killed himself," Patrick admitted, slowly bringing her back to him. "A single gunshot into his brain. He knew you were upstairs and would hear the shot. I personally find that especially cruel of him, and cowardly too."

She had closed her eyes. She found it impossible to keep them open. All she knew was that Patrick was somewhere above her. "I will read it to you if you wish," he said.

"Read what?"

"The note in your father's hand; the police had it. They were kind enough to provide me with a photocopy."

Emily glanced back at her father slumped over his desk, the blood pooling, the note still in his hand. She eventually nodded. "Okay," she agreed quietly.

"This is going to hurt." Patrick read it out aloud from memory.

Dearest Edward,

We've talked about it, talked and talked – and you know I cannot stay. I must go. I don't trust myself to stay. Every time I see her, I want to blame her. I know she is just a child and we were the ones responsible, but I can't help what I feel. And what I feel is this – I hope God can find a suitable punishment for her and that one day I can forgive her. And I hope you can forgive me for this. I never will.

You know I love you, and in my way Emily too.

But sometimes love is simply not enough.

Robin

"That is difficult to take, I know," Patrick said. "But there is more. Your mother is still alive, Emily. She has married again. She lives in New York. She has two children. I have spoken to her."

Emily listened, absorbed, then suddenly tore at her IV. "Unplug me! Fucking unplug me! How could you do this to me, you bastard! Unplug me! Fucking unplug me!"

"Emily...."

Emily wailed. "Shut up! Just shut up! Fucking unplug me! Get this shit out of me! Why are you doing this to me?"

"The truth, Emily; the truth," Patrick insisted quietly.

"Fuck the truth! Fuck it!" she screamed, thrashing on the bed.

Patrick managed to hold her down but only with the help of the others.

"I thought my mother was dead, you bastard!" Emily screamed and fought. "She's alive! Did you think I wouldn't remember?"

"Emily...."

"Ha! Fuck you! Fuck you!"

PURGATORY

"Do you remember anything now?" Patrick asked.

"No, not one thing," Emily said. "Strange, isn't it? I recall so much about you, your life, Francesco, Bekele, and, of course Alessandra. I can carry on a conversation, read a book, know the names of actors in the movies we watch together, but sometimes I can't remember my name, the names of my family, or where I came from. It doesn't seem to matter, though, does it? I mean, I feel I know who I am despite all that."

"That is because you remain Emily. Do you recall the session with the drug? Doctor Ansari, Nurse Kumbahaba?

"No, not really."

"Do you recall us?"

Emily looked up and smiled. "Of course; I wouldn't forget that."

"And my name?"

Emily laughed quietly. "Doctor Marsh, of course – Doctor Patrick Marsh and you are an angel. I was rescued by an angel and this hospital room is heaven!"

"This is not heaven."

"And not hell," Emily insisted, her eyes bright – morphine; it was the only drug that seemed to calm her.

"Something in between, then?" Patrick asked gently.

"Purgatory, with a foot in each?"

Patrick hesitated. "...I suppose that is exactly what our lives are like."

"That is what Alessandra would say," Emily explained, catching Patrick's hesitancy. "We live in purgatory, all of us, one foot in heaven, the other in hell. It is one essential truth of our lives." She added, shifting as the morphine settled her further. "I don't have a mother, you know; maybe Alessandra could be mine; do you think she would if I asked her?"

"But that would make us brother and sister," Patrick offered with a smile.

Emily threw her head back, her laugh only partially suppressed by the morphine. "Ha! That's right! That's hilarious!" She quickly quieted. "Alessandra could tell us those stories of snow forty feet deep and the river ice like black glass that cracks at night, and the stars like diamonds in the night sky. She would kiss us good night and everything would be fine, just fine. We would live forever, you and me." She took a deep breath. "You know, everything seems so bright; there is a glow around everything: you, the light behind you, everything. I feel warm all over; fire rushing through my veins, and I feel good."

ALESSANDRA

Emily, her mind adrift, floating in a sea of nothing, watched Alessandra slowly appear out of the fog.

"Ah, there you are!" Alessandra exclaimed, waving. Her voice was that of an angel's, heaven-sent.

The cab door opened, and Alessandra extended her hand inward. Emily held on tight as she climbed out into the blinding light. She had to shield her eyes; she had forgotten her sunglasses.

"Don't you look lovely today," Alessandra said when she was standing before her. They stood on the sidewalk next to the park, busy traffic flowing past. The cab pulled away.

"I don't feel lovely."

"But you are!"

Once Alessandra had told her, "You, Emily Martina Portinari, are not your beautiful face," while watching her carefully, smiling as Emily blushed. "Beauty is a light in the heart," she had finished, leaning forward, kissing her gently. Emily could feel the heat in her face even now. Alessandra must have noticed how red she had become.

"You are not your body," Alessandra had said too.

"I know, I know...."

Alessandra: beautiful; dark hair falling to her shoulders, grey eyes that swept Emily up into safety and comfort. Emily wanted to say how much she loved her. One does not say such things to one's mother often enough, although Alessandra was not her mother, now, was she? Emily's mother was dead; the same thing had killed her that was now killing Emily – that is what her father had told her.

They navigated the human river arm in arm. Sunlight flooded the street. It was spring.

"How ever did you find me?" Emily asked, confused. Immersed in fog one minute, Alessandra by her side the next; a busy, busy bustling city surrounding them. A gorgeous day.

"Patrick told me about you, and I thought I would find out for myself what you are like. From what he said you are quite a mystery – most unexpected and most welcome, I should add, too. But there is another reason, too, isn't there?"

"What do you think so far? Tell me you like me; I hope you do."

"I like you very much. We are going to be friends for a long time."

Emily pointed to her temple. "But what about up here?"

Alessandra turned her so that they faced one another. "What about that, dear?"

"You wouldn't want a daughter-in-law who is as sick as I am."

"Who says you are sick? You are a lovely girl." They set off again. "Anyway, we will get you right as rain soon enough."

Emily felt herself floating. "How are you going to do that?"

Alessandra shrugged her slim shoulders. "First we work on your body and then we work on your heart." She added more seriously, "But it is up to Patrick, though, too, isn't it? I mean, as clever as he is, he sometimes misses the point, now, doesn't he? I suppose I shall give him a nudge;

that's what mothers are for, aren't they: when all else fails, nudging their sons in the right direction?" She laughed. "He does need the odd nudge sometimes, doesn't he?" she added catching Emily's eye and smiling. "Besides, I'm not too happy with that drug thing he and the others did to you; I will have a chat with him about that when I get the chance. I know that he means well; he always does; he is a good boy; you know that."

"Is he your real son?" Emily demanded to know. "He is not adopted, is he?" Alessandra started with surprise. She turned and studied Emily more closely. "And Francesco is the father? Patrick's real father?" Emily asked.

Alessandra, understanding, cupped Emily's face in her free hand while the other continued to hold tightly onto Emily's. "I will explain all that later," she said softly. "But for now, there are other things to celebrate, are there not?"

Emily turned crimson.

Alessandra smiled. "All other reasons aside, as soon as I learned of it, and how you felt about it, I came as soon as I could."

Emily smiled in response and nodded, feeling found out. "Ah, yes... I wasn't going to say."

"Why ever not, dear; something as important as that? Another life, why wouldn't you say?"

"I don't know."

They continued along the sidewalk. "Do you know what you are going to call her?" Alessandra turned to catch Emily's expression.

Emily continued to blush, her heart rate tripping along. Alessandra would have known about their child all along, of course. "Lizzy, I think. Yes, we have decided on Lizzy... Elizabetta Alessandra," Emily explained, deeply affected, nearly to tears, and proud.

Alessandra reached across and grasped Emily's other hand, holding both. They walked together as if in an embrace, as if dancing as Alessandra laughed like Emily laughed, throwing her head back. "I like that: Elizabetta Alessandra Marsh, a good Italian name!"

Nothing could be hidden from Alessandra and that was a good thing, Emily thought, silently weeping, weeping for all that she was feeling.

"But you didn't have to call her after me, dear," Alessandra added, controlling her smile, keeping it even.

"Why wouldn't I?"

Emily placed her hand on her abdomen. She was almost certain she could feel life stirring. "The bright future is within me," she said. She did not wait for Alessandra's response before adding, knowing she sounded like Patrick, "The past and the future are here." She embraced the life in her, holding it close in the embrace of her hands.

Alessandra recovered her hands, holding them, kissing them, one then the other. "And so it is, my love; and so it is. Elizabetta will be with us forever soon enough."

Emily glimpsed Patrick slipping through the crowd toward them.

"Patrick is here...."

Alessandra looked about, surprised, pleased.

Emily smiled, adjusting her smile and the tip of her head to let Alessandra know she had simply imagined him. Alessandra understood. Alessandra understood more than her son ever could. "*Ahhh...!*" Alessandra sighed, her understanding rising.

Patrick, the ghost of him, was all around, in every face, in the sunlight as it fell across the awning and warmed the red, blue, purple, white, and yellow flowers that filled and spilled out of the pots that led them inside. He was not real, not in body, but in Emily's mind. She felt his presence and that made him real.

He was waiting for them by the door leading into the restaurant. Emily averted her gaze so as not to look at him directly but then unable to resist glanced in his direction. Her heart lifted and leapt as, seemingly detecting her presence, his head began to move in a slow arc toward her.

Emily closed her eyes and then opened them: there was no one there, of course; she knew there would not be. Patrick, the real Patrick, was lying next to her, asleep, and dreaming. He said he dreamed all the time.

"I wonder if your dreams are like my dreams," she had said to him once, quietly adding, "Maybe our dreams are the same – that's possible when people are as connected as we are."

"Why don't I tell him how I feel?" she asked Alessandra.

"How do you feel, exactly?" Alessandra said.

"I don't know…. I feel so much I sometimes don't know what I'm feeling."

"We're all like that sometimes."

"I love him, you know."

"I know."

"He's your son."

Alessandra smiled.

"But at other times I don't feel anything. I sometimes feel as if I'm incapable of feeling anything: nothing true, nothing real."

"That's not true; it cannot be."

"Except for his trek through the desert when his father died – I felt a great deal then: I could have killed him."

"You and the desert and myself as well, my love, to say nothing of his brother who threatened him with worse."

"He tried to kill himself, I think."

"I don't think so, dear. The living never want to join the dead; they only want to be close to them."

Emily ran her fingers along the white tablecloth, feeling the heavy texture, sensing how it had been sun and wind dried. She lifted the heavy cloth napkin, unfolded it, caressed it, and settled it across her lap. *Carmelo's* was crowded, warm and full of the smells of wonderfully delicious food.

She ordered a Caesar salad accompanied by freshly baked bread and bottle of Valpolicella – not too dry. Alessandra ordered the same, brisk and quick, her smiling eyes all the while fastened on Emily. Alessandra was alive and real and not just a figment of her imagination. Her smile enveloped Emily like a protective blanket.

"It's all coming back to you, isn't it?" Alessandra said. "If you feel like you do at this moment then it must be so."

Emily felt a rush of heat flush her face leaving behind a thin layer of perspiration across her forehead. "Many things are coming back," she replied, reaching up and tracing a finger across her brow. "It feels so real."

Alessandra returned the pressure of Emily's grasp and smiled, "It is a good thing," she said and they each quietly laughed.

Alessandra is unaffectedly beautiful, Emily thought.

Her soul and mind.

The waiter returned with a basket of hot bread wrapped in a heavy napkin. He passed it close and then stepped back. The heat and aroma prompted Emily to nearly laugh aloud. She threw her head back. She instead wept, wiping at her eyes as she reached for the bread. "The simplest things seem to do that to me. Does it ever happen to you, Alessandra?"

"Oh yes, dear, all the time: happy things, sad things equally. Do we not all feel the same? Do I not feel what you feel? Are we not all human?"

Emily held the hot bread by the tips of her fingers, passing it quickly from one set of fingers to another. She smeared the bread with butter and then plunged it into her mouth, another piece followed by another. A trickle of melted butter ran down her chin.

"Il pane è la vita stessa!" Alessandra mused from across the table.

Emily glanced up, surprised, and, caught out, laughed with Alessandra, politely covering her mouth before guiltily shoving in yet another piece. "You speak Italian!"

"As do you, my love – but I can barely understand you! You are speaking with your mouth full!"

Emily managed to swallow, and immediately slipped in yet another piece of bread equally slathered in warmed butter.

"Ha!"

A glow surrounded everything and everyone: the sunlight through the window, the voices lifting and falling, the deep rich scents, the colors, and the very fabric of the air. The sounds of the restaurant, like music, followed the synchronized beating of all the souls: it was a busy sound, a warm sound. Emily turned to look about – and a face lifted, and another, and then all that were there turned toward her, their eyes meeting hers in a moment of understanding, of acknowledgment, of wonder; and, above all, of kindness.

It's what makes the world work, kindness; that and the common bond that binds us all together – our humanity. Alessandra had told her that, long ago. She had known Alessandra forever, it often seemed.

It is true, too.

Emily recalled how, once, Alessandra had sat in the cane-backed chair beside her bed, leaning forward, her legs crossed, her elbow on her knee, her chin resting upon the heel of her hand as she smiled and composed her stories of glacial winters, frantic springs, and summers that lasted forever. She remembered how she lay in her bed with her head on the pillow listening, her mind in the world of Alessandra's making, her body safe beneath the coolness of the cotton sheets. Alessandra told her of her perfect world, her Village of the Heart, where we all go, she said, when the day is done, and night is upon us.

"In dreams, Alessandra?"

"Yes, my love, in dreams."

"I'm dreaming you now," Emily stated evenly and lightly addressing Alessandra sitting across the table from her.

Alessandra squeezed her hand. All this time, from climbing up out of the cab, entering the restaurant, to sitting at the table, she had not let go.

"I feel as if I'm floating but I don't know where I am going half the time. Do you know where all this is heading? Where am I going?"

"Wherever your heart may take you, my love; wherever your heart may take you."

Emily laughed, then wept, joyous tears coursing down her cheeks. "I could stay in this dream forever," she said, "as long as you were in it!"

DROWNING

Emily grasped the windowsill and looked out into the night searching out the shadowed places, light and dark. They had been lying side by side in her bed, she listening to his voice through his chest, his steady breathing, and the rhythmic beating of his heart. It always seemed to be that way; it was a pattern that she was quite used to. He had received a call; he had to go. The life of a medical doctor, and a good one.

He had not gone yet, though, and Emily turned to him. She stood naked.

"My sister's name was Elizabetta," she said. "Elizabetta Giovanna Portinari. She was named after my grandmother on my father's side, long dead now."

"I'm glad you remember. It has been a struggle, I know," Patrick said, preparing to get dressed.

"I look better, don't you think? I feel better," she said facing him, opening her arms, palms out, presenting herself.

Patrick returned her smile and slowly nodded.

She sat on the edge of the bed. "But why does all this matter anyway?" she asked. "We should never look back, isn't that right? We should always look ahead."

"The past is important," Patrick said evenly, continuing to dress, more quickly now, determined to leave her. "It defines us: good and bad, sad and joyful. How can we know where we are going if we don't understand from where we have come?"

"Do you remember what I told you about the dream I had last night?"

"I remember."

"It seemed so real – But it is often hard to tell what is real and what is not, isn't it?"

"Very much so."

"I was having a baby – do you know what I called her?"

"I can guess. Was I the father?"

Emily smiled. "Who do you think?" She smiled again. "So, what comes next is the sad part, isn't it? I mean when I finally remember what happened to Elizabetta it will be sad, won't it?" Her smile dropped off as she asked.

Patrick lay her back on the bed and kissed her. "Perhaps you should get some sleep," he said softly. "We can talk about all this in the morning when I return."

"My mother, too. There is something sad about her, too, isn't there? I can't remember my mother's name. What was her name again?"

"I'm sure it will come to you."

"That's not fair; if you told me, my memories of her would come flooding back. You told me my father's name; it's Edward; he doesn't like Eddie, or Ed. He only goes for Edward. He likes the formality, I think. He is a rather formal man. He dresses well."

"I only met him that one time. He had some style, that is certain. He was very handsome in the same way you are beautiful."

"Where is my father, by the way? I haven't seen him for a while."

Patrick was dressed now and preparing to go.

"I said something that wasn't right, didn't I?" Emily asked, noticing the expression on his face. He cupped her chin in his hand. "We will clear it all up when I get back," he again promised.

"If you say so," Emily replied trying to make light of it. She suddenly gasped. "Oh, wait I remember!" Her memory caught and held. "Oh God, I know why I have not seen him; he's dead. How could I forget! You must think I'm totally crazy!"

"I don't."

"I called 911, didn't I?"

"You did." Patrick grasped her hand and kissed it. "It's okay."

Emily nodded briskly. "I know it is."

"Get some sleep; I will be back soon. Soon, I promise."

"So you say... so you say," she said, teasing him with a pained smile and a roll of her eyes.

Patrick departed, leaving her at fast pace out the bedroom door. Down the stairs; the front door unlocked; stepping through; the door closing and then locked. She waited, not moving. She heard the car start then pull out, and the room already deep in shadow darkened with only the sound of her breathing and the ringing in her ears in contrast to the exact and precise silence of her dead father's house.

Emily stepped into the river. Silver and gold, green and blue, white and black. Movement straight and fast, oblique and darting, swirling and turning. Reflections light and dark, perfect mirrors, perfect invisibility; and, of course, life and death, beauty, adjacent to the stagnant mélange of mud and root.

She pushed along the shoreline, mud between her toes, sticks and swirls of pollen about her shins. The river was deeper than she thought and the current stronger. She stumbled, just managing to remain upright. She carelessly leaned forward to see beyond the shiny surface, lifting the hem of her dress with one hand, keeping her hair in place with the other. A tadpole, black and long-tailed with early signs of arms and legs, and small fish darting between the stones black and green and quick; golden flakes from the gravel bed; a crayfish, a water spider. Standing, straightening, she faced a bulrush with its heavy stalk and club of brown felt.

She glanced back over her shoulder; Elizabetta sat on the bank with her toes in the water. Emily pulled out a stalk, yanking hard, and pushed through the river to her sister's side, and ran the soft stock against her cheek just so she could feel the softness. Her sister had blonde hair not unlike her own hair. Her eyes, not unlike her own. The shape of her mouth, the sweep of her chin. "Bulrushes; that's a bulrush," Emily patiently explained. "Some call them Cattails."

She turned back to the river and waded out further. "Water lily," she explained, pointing. She picked the yellow flower and held it up. "One for you and one for me...." Emily reached for another, reached too far, and was abruptly beneath the surface. How odd the world had suddenly become; cold, and quiet, and not quite real. She opened her eyes just in time to see Elizabetta glide across the blue and white of what must have been the sky.

Emily's feet found the stone bed and she stood, coughing out the river, pushing her hair back. It wasn't deep at all; the river was barely up to her waist. She looked around. Elizabetta was receding into the distance face-down in the river. In another moment, she turned a corner and was gone. Elizabetta was gone. It was if Elizabetta Giovanna Portinari had never existed.

Emily covered her face and wept. She wept until Patrick returned hours later. It was nearly dawn.

"It was the same day as the picnic, you know," Emily explained later in the day when she felt she could. "We went to find my mother to let my father sleep. We didn't wake him; we snuck away. My mother said she was going down to the river and that's where we went, Elizabetta and me. My mother is dead, too, you know; the same disease as me." Emily tapped her head. "It runs in the family, you see; Elizabetta, then my mother, and now me – although Elizabetta drowned, I know now. Life in our family is death anyway you look at it. What was my mother's name again, I seem to have forgotten?"

"Robin."

"Just Robin?"

"Robin Marie Portinari; her maiden name was Vaughan."

"She was tall?"

"She is as tall as you."

"Color of her hair?"

"Blonde, like yours."

"Green eyes?"

"Yes."

Emily absently traced the outline of her cheek and chin, her eyes fastened on Patrick. "Her chin?"

"Similar – though she is like you through the eyes mostly, I think."

"I thought so. It is sad – but it is okay now."

"How is that?"

"Because I have Alessandra now – and you, of course."

Patrick nodded and smiled sadly in agreement.

"Of course."

I AM MY BODY

Two bodies, wrapped together, eyes closed, catching their breath, sweat and ecstasy, a young woman and a young man.

"So...."

"So...."

Emily propped herself up. "Hmmm...."

"Hmmm.... What?" Patrick asked opening his eyes.

"That was good, don't you think?"

He brushed back her hair. "I do."

"I've had a thought."

"Oh, Oh."

"Maybe we are our bodies after all – what do you think?"

Patrick thought about it then shook his head without commenting.

Emily continued. "I mean, what did we just experience? I mean, look what my body has done to me; my body is killing me!" She tapped her forehead. "That thing in my head, you know?" She continued without pausing, turning in the bed to face him. "We are born just tiny things, not knowing anything, barely the sound of our mother's voice. We grow and learn thanks to a functioning brain; without one, of course.... Our bodies change. We crave sex; most of us – but there are always exceptions to the rule, aren't there, but they are not going anywhere, are they? We have babies who are the future, as our bodies, the job done, slowly wither; no more sex; unable to reproduce, anyway. And all that only if you're lucky; the unlucky ones go quick, but we all go, isn't that right?"

"You are not going anywhere, and nor am I, not anytime soon, anyway."

"How do you know?"

"I know."

"How?"

He thought. "Of course, I don't know but I have faith that we will or why continue?"

Emily threw her legs off the edge of the bed and stood. She leaned forward and kissed him then slowly straightened, looking down. "What are you smiling about?" she asked smiling back, tipping her head.

"How beautiful you are."

"Is that funny?"

"No."

She pulled on her housecoat, threading her arms through, wrapping the gown around her and tying it off at the waist. She sat on the edge of the bed and took his hand. "I feel good – you have really helped me. But I am afraid." She thought a moment then stood and made her way to the dresser. She selected a string of pearls that were laying out and ready, then returned and sat, extending them.

"Do you mind?"

He undid the clasp, opened the string, then, stretching, positioned the pearls around her neck. She watched him through half closed eyes, the dark hair, his dark eyes following the end of the string.

"They were my grandmother's, on my mother's side," she explained softly, caressing the soft inside of his wrist with her cheek. "I remember her giving them to me. It was my graduation. Her name was Ruthie."

"There now," he said, sitting back, the clasp closed. "They are very elegant, but what is more important is that you can recall from where they came; that is very promising. Perhaps we are over the worst, turning the tide."

Emily traced and retraced the length of pearls with the tips of her fingers. "I remember some things, but very little really," she said slowly. "It is frustrating, maddening. There is you – I remember you from yesterday, and the day before, and the day before. It is the same with Alessandra – but I know she is not real; that is, the Alessandra I imagine is the not the real Alessandra, is she? The Alessandra I know is, as you say, a confabulation I created because I recall no one else, not even my own mother. There is Elizabetta – again, I know, not real but another confabulation as you call her. Elizabetta died long ago – drowned but not my fault." Emily continued to run her fingers over the string of pearls. "My father – his name escapes me; funny how I can't remember that – killed himself, didn't he? Blew his brains out. I called 911 and then passed out."

"Edward."

"Yes, Edward. My mother's name –wait, it is coming to me.... ...Rose?"

"Robin."

"Ah! And, as you told me on more than one occasion, I live in Montreal on Rue St Urbain. The St Lawrence is the river that flows past the city toward the ocean. There is something about rivers, you know.... I have some kind of affinity for rivers, the dark and deep kind. I don't know why that is, do you? Anyway, the mountains in the distance are the Laurentians, and this is my father's house. It is mine now, I suppose. Why did he blow his brains out? He was my father; fathers don't do that sort of thing."

"He saw no future, I suppose. He had no faith in what the future could be."

Emily turned to the mirror and again felt along the length of pearls. "I'm feeling rather weak. ...You said I would," she said quietly, speaking to her reflection. She turned to him. "It is not over yet, is it?"

"Time will tell."

"Oh, yeah, right," she said quietly. *"Shhh! Listen!"* She lifted her hand requesting he listen too. "The tapping against the window – it is raining out." She shifted to the window, taking long strides, and peeked out through the curtains. It was snowing. Sleet tapped the glass. "I can hear it against the pane, can you?" she asked hushed, mesmerized by the scene of driving snow and sleet, her expression drawn.

Patrick joined her by the window, the bedsheet wrapped around him toga-like. He grasped her hand, and drawing it to him, allowed the curtain to drop. "You must be freezing," he said gently as he scooped her up and carried her back to the bed.

Another day. Another month. Her pearls safely on the dresser top; their clothes scattered across the floor in their rush toward their bed. Her barrette tangled in her hair. Nearly dawn.

"You know all about Alessandra, don't you?" Emily asked. "I mean, you know all about Alessandra and me."

"Alessandra, again." Patrick shook his head and sighed, not frustrated but resigned.

Emily smiled. "There is nothing to worry about, but I can understand how you might feel the way you do. We are, after all, talking about your mother, aren't we? It must seem very personal."

Patrick checked his response.

"Alessandra and I are lovers," Emily stated flatly, studying his reaction. Once captured, she tipped her head and smiled. "You did not know?"

"You and my mother are lovers?"

"Yes, that's right; does it shock you?"

"I have to say it does."

"We are lovers in the finest sense of the word."

Patrick studied her wondering what she might say next. "You're teasing me," he said.

Emily slowly shook her head. "No...." She kept her smile. "Tell me about Alessandra falling in love...," she demanded suddenly. "I want to know all the details, notwithstanding the fact that the love her life – your father – he is your real father, isn't he? – is no longer with us."

"It was a singular moment, a pinpoint in time in the depths of winter, a perfect winter, in a perfect cold, the coldest she had ever experienced up until then, and since," he quickly said without having to think of what to say. He was well prepared; she had asked the same many times previously.

"Uh-huh," Emily agreed nodding slowly.

"There was the river...," Patrick added.

"Yes, the river.... Keep going."

"...And it was frozen right across, the ice marble green and so transparent you could see through to the bottom to the weeds and the motionless fish suspended, as if hanging from a thread fastened to the ice above. She and my father skated all day following the length of the river, skating on and on, skating until their legs felt like wooden sticks, and their ankles broken. Soon night was approaching, and before they knew it, the night snuck up on them and it became pitch black with only the stars and a thin strip of white where the snow lay on the bank to guide them."

"I can see the thread of snow on the banks against the black ice," Emily replied in wonder. "I can hear the ice crack!" She smiled quietly.

Patrick continued. "The ice had become a mirror, Heaven above and below them. They held hands as they pirouetted beneath the echoed stars. They danced until they felt warm and then stood back-to-back looking upward, slowly turning in place, and gathering in heaven as it spiralled above their heads and wrapped about their feet.... And you are right; the ice cracked; the ice cracked as they kissed for the first time."

Emily closed her eyes as she imagined it. "I like that: the ice cracked as they kissed for the first time."

"Does your love affair with my mother include kissing?"

She turned to him and smiled. "What a question."

He waited patiently, uncertain what Emily might say next, uncertain he wanted to hear it.

"Okay, then – yes, if you really want to know; all the time, in fact; whenever I'm scared, or lonely, or just sad. When life gets difficult – you know what I mean by that, don't you? I think you do – I climb into her bed and she puts her arm around me, and I can sleep."

Patrick slowly nodded his understanding. "I thought so."

Emily considered then abruptly asked, "Is there any hot chocolate in this tale of a frozen river? Please tell me there is."

"Is this a test of some sort or are you once again

teasing me?"

Emily's smile opened. "Both."

"Buckets of it."

"With marshmallows?"

"Spilling over the edge of their mugs, sticking to their fingers; they had to lick them clean so they could put their gloves back on."

"I want to feel like they felt," Emily said with a sigh. "I want to belong like that." She sat up, leaned over him and then kissed him. She kissed him once more before lying back. "Come here," she said, drawing him to her, wrapping herself around him.

"Do you love me?" she asked.

"More than life."

SNOWING

Emily walked a few paces back along the path lined with overhanging clematis before suddenly turning around. She smoothed the creases of her dress and pushed back an errant lock of hair that had fallen out from behind her ear.

"How do I look?"

"Like the sun," Alessandra said as she quietly closed the big doors, leaving Emily alone in the garden.

Emily stepped through the open gate, pushing aside the strands of clematis that reached as low as her bare shoulders and swept over her face. She carefully closed the gate behind her ensuring it was latched and stepped out along the forest path toward where Alessandra suggested he might be waiting, picking up her pace as she went along. Directionless light filtered through the reaching canopy filling the dark spaces surround her. The individual leaves immediately above her remained in shadow but looking upward and beyond where sunlight caught the edges, the foliage resembled a cluster of emeralds and glistening silver.

She managed the clearing beside the brook and came to a halt. Nothing of the outside world intruded; completely silent if one measured the degree of silence by the lack of manmade sound. The sound of her blood rushing in her ears and the faint sound of her heartbeat; birdsong, the gentle turning leaves, a nearby brook gathered in the greater hush. Her eyes followed the cascade of green and light down to where the true mystery began: the dark life, where the fallen leaves lay, where earth is made, where all things are possible.

"Emily?"

She jumped.

"I thought I lost you for a moment," he said, slowly approaching.

"I am not lost, far from it."

He offered his hand. She accepted it.

"Are you all right?"

"Why wouldn't I be?"

"No reason." He looked around then back to her and smiled. "I startled you."

She shrugged and smiled and shook her head prettily. "No, not really."

He teased her. "So, you are attuned to the forest, with every one of your senses finely honed to hear and know each rustling sound, crack of twig, rustle of branch?"

"Of course," she said remaining careful.

"So?"

"...So?"

"Is there a chance you might recognize me?"

"Of course!" She quickly added, "But I don't know your name, and how could I, you have not properly introduced yourself, have you?"

"We do know one another, and quite well at that."

She fumbled her response, blushing wildly. In the end she did not respond but continued to blush, nervously looking away.

"You do know my name, don't you? It is in there somewhere. Give it a try. I'm sure you will recall it, and then your own name, too."

"I know my name."

"What is it?"

Emily took a deep breath. She let it out slowly. "Emily."

"Right, and mine?"

"What do you mean by right? You cannot tell me *I'm right* about my own name? Who do you think you are!"

"So what is my name?"

She took another breath, held it, then released. "Patrick."

"Right again – but, then again, what is in a name? It is who you feel you are inside that is more important. Whatever name you might say, I could only agree."

"That sounds like bullshit to me. You are Patrick and I am Emily!"

"Right."

"Please don't say *right* again!" A sudden flood of memories filled Emily up. She staggered. "I remember the scent of you," she breathed, recovering quickly. "Oh my God!"

Patrick held her and kissed her lips lightly and with her memory quickly cemented, she responded, returning his kiss.

She straightened, smiled, more confident, rearranging her dress; "Oh, right, it's you." She laughed weakly. "Right? Right."

"Right."

"Oh God! Stop that! But I hope I did not embarrass you this time!"

"Not especially. Do you recall where we are?"

Emily shook her head, still finding her feet.

"The Arboretum for the afternoon; you always wanted to go, and here we are."

She looked around taking in the close press of forest. "Oh! yes! I see...."

"Look up."

She tipped her head back, almost losing her balance. He kept her steady. "Ha! There's glass! We are inside!" She raised a quick hand. *"Shhh! Listen! It is snowing out!"* She continued to listen then whispered, "I can hear ice crystals tapping on the glass...." She glanced at him and straightened. "I have been here before: *Déjà vu.*"

"You are thinking of another time; the top floor of your father's house a few days ago; you and I looking out the window."

She slowly nodded, recalling the moment, at least in part.

They strode arm in arm along a stone path that meandered beneath overhanging bougainvillea, wild fig, kapok, and eucalyptus. A blue-throated bee-eater fluttered through the foliage: wings pressing, feathers hollowing the flight, a body lighter than air ducking and weaving. The sound of trickling water flowing from somewhere above, dropping onto and trailing over moss-covered rocks into darkened pools lined with leaves blackened with age. A small lizard scurrying over fallen leaves looking for the dark, secret places beneath ragged rocks dripping with moisture and covered with moss. They wandered through a thriving and vibrant tropical forest, dripping with water and life, protecting and enfolding those silent hidden things that would soon blossom and tower upward.

The garden existed primarily because the underlying structure and mechanisms of life made it so, but it also existed because it was held protected beneath its dome of glass, and because the men and women who nurtured it did so more out of love than out of duty. It could not exist within the full glory of its means without this duality. Men and women are responsible for their world; they are the custodians, not some unnamed god.

"Do you know what I'm thinking?" she asked.

"I do not."

Emily reached for the limb of a tropical flower – white plumeria. She brought it up to smell, brushing the soft petals against her cheek before setting it gently aside.

"I know what you are thinking," she said.

"And what is that?"

"How gorgeous it is here – how very *necessary* it all is."

She slowly turned about with her arms extended, her head cast back, her eyes closed. Patrick caught her as she came around a second time. "I think I am not meant to know my past, not any single part of it, only the merely mundane and automatic, the mechanical parts," she said. "That part of me, which I do not remember, is gone forever. In some way, I have never existed, not really." She twirled around again. "But, today, today I am reborn! The future awaits, and I look forward to it!"

He steadied her, stopping her from falling.

"Woo, I'm dizzy! ...But...but...but can you smell the lilac? It fills the world," she offered.

He thought a moment then said, "I can; it is very fragrant."

She settled, composing herself, and then looked up at him. "We're making progress here, don't you think?" she asked evenly. "...But now I sound like you, I suppose, don't I?" She kissed his shoulder, rested her forehead against it, and then looked up again. "Are you crying?"

"No, of course not."

"Your eyes are red."

She took a deep breath, drawing herself up.

"...Patrick," she said slowly, drawing his name out, looking up again as if she might be intoxicated, slightly unsteady. "I like saying your name."

She waited, weaving. "...Nothing to say?"

He shook his head.

"Cat got your tongue for a change?"

"I don't know, does it?"

They listened to the hidden silence together.

"It is very quiet," Emily offered unnecessarily after a moment, lightly jabbing him with her elbow.

"A stirring ambiance, I would say," he responded.

It was game they played.

"A beautiful day."

"Most excellent."

"Gorgeous."

"Lovely."

"Absolutely amazing."

"Stunningly brilliant."

"Absolutely most incredible, I would say," Emily finished and again quickly lifted her hand asking for silence. "Can you hear it? Ice pellets on the glass? It is snowing out."

"I hear it."

"I won't forget that sound. It is in such contrast to inside, isn't it? I will never forget it."

"But what will you think," she asked, continuing; "what will you do tomorrow when I won't remember you? What will become of me then? More important, what will become of you?"

"I am not important."

"You are to me. ...Do you love me?"

"More than life."

Emily threw her head back and laughed. "Ha! I have you well trained!" She settled. "...But please don't ever forget me. That's what's important, at least to me it is."

"Not in a million years."

"A million years?" Emily nodded, considering. "...That's good, good; a million years of remembering is not exactly forgetting, is it?" She placed her hand on his arm and smiled. "I will take it. Thank you."

FACETIME

Patrick had received a text from Alessandra earlier saying that the village finally had internet. They had joined the world. Not that everyone was happy about it. But one can't, or at least shouldn't, stick one's head in the sand, should one? So Alessandra said.

Alessandra called him first. Patrick was at his desk preparing his files for the day. It was nine in the morning. He answered her FaceTime call using his laptop; she used her phone, held at arms' length, gazing into it.

Patrick smiled and then laughed in surprise. "Hey!"

"How are you doing?" Alessandra laughed back. "Look at me! Look at you!"

Patrick grinned. "I see you! A true Luddite shedding her shackles!"

Alessandra played with her hair, tossing it back. "I must look a wreck...."

Long dark hair tied back with no trace of grey revealing her ears with jade earrings. No makeup – perhaps just a touch – and smiling blue eyes. All in proportion. Yes, a hint of lipstick, Patrick noted, and perhaps a hint of eyeshadow too.

"You look fine; it is you for sure."

Alessandra laughed again, contagiously as always. "Thanks very much for that!"

Patrick laughed with her. She was as quick as ever. And classically beautiful, too; he wondered how she did it. "It is good to see you!" he said. He knew her birthday, but not the year; she had managed to somehow keep it secret all these years. But she had to be at least sixty; she looked mid-forties.

"And you too! ...I like this, don't you? I have not seen you in such a long while, and here I am looking right at you! I know we've talked but it is not the same, is it? Tell you what, after this, I'm calling Bekele – but I have to be careful of the time difference; I made that mistake once before. Once I called and woke him up and it was three in the morning his time!" She threw her head back and laughed; just like Emily, Patrick thought, surprised by the similarity. He quickly recovered.

"I have been meaning to call you," he said, meaning it.

"Of course, you have!" Alessandra stretched to see over his shoulder. "Is that the St Lawrence down there?" Patrick acknowledged it was without turning. "It is open in part – fast moving, I would guess." She studied the scene more fully. "Move your head a bit...And the hills beyond are at least partially snow-covered." She panned the phone to show him the scene through her kitchen window: a snow scape of glacial capped mountains etched into a sky of unearthly blue.

"It snowed again last night," she said. She switched the camera back so that she once again filled the screen. "It is not that cold – well, yes, it is cold but not all that bad. You have to dress right; mittens and boots and toques, and all that. Bekele would hate it here; you might survive, being from Montreal, and what a great city it is too."

"I'm not from Montreal. I am only here temporarily."

"You are a Canadian!"

He teased her in turn. "Most Canadians go south this time of year."

"Where are you going, then?"

"Home."

"This is your home now! Here! Take the next plane out; you would be home by tomorrow... well, maybe the day after tomorrow. I could arrange for someone to pick you and Emily up in Castlegar, whisk you both here in a wink! They know all the back roads. Bundle you and Emily up and pack you in, so to speak!"

"You have retreated to the ends of the earth, mother; the ends of the earth. I would not be able to get there for a month. When the snow melted, maybe, and only maybe."

"Not true, not true! But it is true we have fought long and hard to keep it that way for a long time. Still, I insisted we get internet. One has to catch up occasionally." She smiled with the absurdity of what she was saying. "And that is another reason really why I'm calling, not just for you to gaze upon my aging self, and not only because I wanted to see how you might be doing." She kept her eyes locked with her son's. "To see that you are still good, and it appears as if you are." Her smile shifted. "A little worried about something.... I can guess about who. Not me, or your brother."

She abruptly changed course, following the thread. "By the way, Bekele is living in our old home now, you know," she said. "He won't be coming out here any time soon, I would guess, and that is unfortunate. I sold it to him," she added, keeping her smile while waiting for Patrick to respond.

Patrick knew all about it; Bekele had called to ensure he was okay with it.

"Old news – Bekele called and told me. Reverse charges; I accepted."

"That was nice of you. Bekele is nearly completely broke, I know. Still, I hope you don't mind. And, and I know this is not news either, but in case you don't know Bekele is going back to school. He's going to be a millwright. No more going to sea for him, thank God. I know you sent him money for that, Patrick; and I know he thanked you every which way. But I want to thank you too; it was and is very generous of you. I know you are not exactly loaded either; you are still a student, I know, despite the fact you have graduated."

Patrick was fully aware of the details. He wondered where all this was going. She had not called him to tell him what he already knew.

"By the way, do you know that Bekele imagined that he was saved by an angel as well as, of course, the crew of the helicopter and the navy ship?"

That's where this was going.

"He wouldn't tell you; he would know what you would think. He told me that she was beautiful like angels are supposed to be beautiful: young, bright-blue eyes, blonde hair swept back held in place by a diamond. She offered her hand and he was suddenly free, flying through the air on the end of a tether. The helicopter winched him in. Soaking wet, of course; frightened out of his wits, but alive."

"The presence of an angel sounds unlikely but everything else seems to add up."

"Of course, it is entirely silly. Who believes in angels these days? But, then again, I do not know what I would think or imagine if I was hanging on the end of a tether in the midst of a November gale being dunked occasionally in one of those big green waves. I thank God he is still alive whatever the reason."

She switched again.

"Lean in a little closer, will you, Patrick? Ah…. Your scar has healed rather nicely, hasn't it? You can hardly tell now." She sat back.

"It was over three years ago."

"Yes, of course, I do remember." She leaned forward again. "I have some sad news, I'm afraid. Aferwicki ibn Mohammed Kadhafo, a good man at the bottom of himself, and, I know, a friend of yours – more than a friend, I know only too well – has died, suddenly, and not in a nice way. He was shot by Eritrean rebels in a case of mistaken identity. If you can believe that."

Patrick took a moment to absorb what Alessandra was telling him. He managed to say his name: "Aferwicki…."

"You know what your father was like with names."

"Yes, I do." He gave the man the respect he deserved and said his full name aloud: *"Aferwicki ibn Mohammed Kadhafo.* It is quite a shock," he added, meaning it, feeling the loss.

"Again, I am sorry, Patrick. It will take you a while, I know." She shifted her phone to her other hand. "In the meantime, there is another reason, which you have probably already guessed, that I felt I should call. Please don't ask me why, but I feel it is imperative that you bring Emily here, Patrick, and as soon as humanly possible."

Patrick straightened, not prepared. "Here? To you? The village?"

"Yes. Do not ask me why."

"Why?"

She ignored her son's gentle jab. "By the way, what were you going to call me about if I had not called you?"

"You seem to be able to read my mind, so you tell me."

"Come on, Patrick; I'm not that bad. You know I have

good reasons for what I do and what I ask."

"I have some trouble following you, Alessandra; what is this all about?"

"Do go on, Patrick; it is your turn." She smiled.

Patrick buried his face in his hands. He dropped them and sighed. He couldn't win. "Emily has had a relapse," he said. "She is not doing well." He had managed to keep his expression frozen while feeling his chest tighten. Alessandra was always full of surprises, to say nothing of determined.

He continued slowly. "It is a very strange situation: extraordinary, really," he began. "Emily has concocted or, I should say, confabulated an incredible version of reality that is not remembered like facts are remembered, or the past is remembered, but as a book or movie is remembered. She cannot recall her own mother, but she does recall almost everything I have told her about you, Francesco, and even Bekele. And you should know, too, that Emily feels she has a special connection with you. It is very unusual, and I don't know why, exactly, she is like that. It can be a little unsettling."

Alessandra settled slightly in her chair. She otherwise made no comment.

"I can see you are not surprised," Patrick said.

"I'm not, but please keep going."

Patrick slowly nodded. "Right–. The micro-fibrous tumor in her brain is continuing to spread. As her ability to remember continues to regress, she is living more and more in her confabulated world. Pretty soon the growth will affect autonomous regions; she is already feeling weak, and she is often disoriented and dizzy. She has had a number of seizures. There is absolutely nothing I or anyone else can do to slow the progress or otherwise turn things around for her, it seems."

"You do know what Emily wants, don't you?" Alessandra asked.

"She wants to belong," he immediately replied, knowing.

"Then it is very important that you bring her home here, and as soon as possible. ...But I have said that already, have I not? Is there any need to repeat myself? There seems there might be." Alessandra tipped her head, very much like Emily, Patrick thought, again taken aback by the similarity.

"But what can we accomplish by taking her on a lengthy and perhaps even dangerous trip through the mountains in her condition," he asked. "That and the fact I cannot just spirit Emily away. She is a patient under my care and to a large extent a ward of the hospital. They know her condition. It would never be allowed. But what I really do not understand is how transferring Emily to Heart, British Columbia could possibly help the situation in any way. Even if it was possible, the trip would likely kill her; it certainly would not help her condition any."

"She wants to go home, Patrick, but first she needs a home. Her home will be here with us – with you too."

"I am trying to save her life, Alessandra! That's all I want to do." His voice cracked at the end.

"Poor Patrick. You are so over your head in this. I know you love her; it is written all over you. We must bring an end to this not only for Emily's sake but for your sake as well, don't we?"

"I don't know what to do."

"You are almost there, Patrick; you are almost there.

Open your mind. In a case like this the extraordinary requires the extraordinary, don't you think?"

"I don't know what to think."

"My poor boy – you know all about the do's and don'ts of the *Danakil*. If this does not turn out well, do not walk there again. Do not be tempted. Please, for all our sakes."

She abruptly broke the connection – searching out the red button, trying twice, failing, smiling, shrugging, then finding the right one and leaving Patrick knowing exactly what she meant but not how his mother could possibly impose the extraordinary upon the inevitable. A few moments later he received a text.

"Please don't worry. Chin up! We will get through this." She appended a smiley face.

ELIZABETTA

Emily opened her eyes. He was standing over her; she could feel his hand in her hand. She returned the pressure.

"What the hell?"

"You have had a seizure."

"Not again."

"Again."

"I remember you leaving the room. How long were you gone?"

"Only for a few minutes."

"It seemed like forever – years. I can barely recall your name it was so long ago." She tried to smile.

"What is my name?"

"Just kidding, Doctor Marsh; I know it's you, so don't pretend you're not who I say you are. Do you know who I am is probably a better question. You know," she said, drawing his hand to her, "and this is odd, I think, don't you? I was looking down at myself; hovering over myself. What do think that means?"

"Out of body experiences are quite common; more than you might think. Or you could simply have been dreaming. We were monitoring your heart rate, breathing, and brain function the entire time and you were not ever in any danger."

"It was weird."

"I can only imagine."

"It was not just that – it was like a parallel world almost, as if I was not really me, or me in another reality." Emily looked about the room. "I'm thirsty, parched. Where is that water you always have around?" Patrick recovered the glass from her bedside table and helped her sit up.

"Ah, so cold – how do you keep it so cold?"

"I always ensure the ice is topped up for you, and the staff are excellent here too."

"Hmmm...." Emily thought then smiled, keeping her eyes on him. "I remember the moment our baby was conceived – Lizzy. Is there anybody in close range? I hope not. What I want to say should only be between me and you."

"We are very much alone. It was a joke; I am the only staff here at the moment. More to the point, there is no baby, Emily. You are not pregnant."

"Oh... There you go again. Spoiler. I just dreamed it, didn't I? I'm still dreaming it and you too."

"I am real, and Elizabetta Alessandra will be perhaps one day but not yet."

"I didn't mean that." She lay her hand on Patrick's arm and smiled. "Are you sure we are alone?"

"Very much so."

"Just yesterday, last night, we were lying on the bed afterward, too dark to see one another. I kissed you and you kissed me. I didn't need to see you; I could feel you. I felt you in me and the surge. I held on; I would not let you go."

Patrick kissed her gently. "Okay."

"Do you remember?" she asked.

Patrick smiled but would not answer. He kissed her again, and then he let her sleep.

The first time Emily looked into Elizabetta Alessandra's eyes her daughter was only two minutes old. She was surprised by their clarity: gray and clear, looking back at her in the same way and with the same curiosity. She was wrapped in a white towel, like swaddling clothes, she thought, with only her face showing. She was weightless in her arms and she held on tight but not too tight for fear she might injure her in some way. She imagined, with a faint horror, how easy it would be for the child to slip through her grip; the slightest unintended gesture on her part and her baby would slip out of her arms with nothing she could do to stop her fall.

She had been told to expect a miracle and there it was, alive, breathing, twisting its miracle face into a scowl, experimenting with the expression, peering off into the distance, then back to her, not quite smiling.

I give you this... I give you all of this... I give you the world, my love!

Emily looked about the room, the effort taking all her strength.

"Where's Patrick?"

Patrick climbed up out of the shadows.

The ache in Emily's body reached up from her core, a deep fathomless ache: to split herself apart like that – first there was one, then two, a child; someone new in the world and all the changes that would bring, new worlds, new beginnings.

She handed Elizabetta to Patrick, watched as he held their child close as she had done, snuggling her up beneath his chin as if he, too, might be afraid of losing his grip on her. She watched him kiss their child and hold her; kiss her and hold her, and then, instantly it seemed, the child was once again in her arms, lying across her breast. Emily kissed and kissed again the soft face with features a shadow of her and some of Patrick, but mostly an individual, fully and completely. She followed Patrick's pattern of kisses and then lifting her eyes to find him, captured his smile. She wondered if he could detect the bottomless exhaustion that nearly consumed her, as much as the love that poured from her and filled the physical distance between them.

And in the cold stone interior of the church, Emily lifted Elizabetta from the baptismal font and named her, *Elizabetta Alessandra Marsh*. She held her child close, her small warm head tucked up tight beneath her chin. She felt a deep resolve settle in her as she made herself and Elizabetta a promise.

"I will love you always."

Alessandra, standing between them, drew Emily and her grandchild close. She whispered, *"Ahhh...,"* kissing Emily, then the child, adding, "she will be with us forever." She kissed Emily again, and again Elizabetta, and then Patrick, quickly, on his cheek. "You, too, then...." She smiled up at her son, her hand lingering on his cheek, turning back to Emily and the child before letting her hand fall away.

"We're going home now," Alessandra said in a voice that carried along the aisles of the stone church, the corners of the transept, into the vestry, throughout the recesses framed by the stained glass, and high up into the arched ceiling. She led the four of them away from the altar and walked them down the aisle between the joyfully weeping men, women, and children, toward the open sun-filled doors of the church, toward the burgeoning God-given world beyond.

"Emily... Hey!"

Gasp. A deep breath. Her body arching in the bed.

"...Ha!"

"Open your eyes."

Emily rolled onto her back. "What happened?"

"Another seizure."

"It is so dark in here – turn on a light."

Patrick obliged her, dropping back onto the bed beside her.

"Look how close we are," Emily said, facing him. "Only a thin film of sweat separates us. That's really nice, I like it. We cannot get any closer than this, can we? This is the ultimate, isn't it: body to body? ...I know what you are going to say, but nope, nope; admit it that this is pretty nice, isn't it?

"It is pretty nice."

"Ha!" She poked him and said softly, "Gotcha!" She kissed him lightly on his lips, her eyes fluttering, barely conscious. "Did I say anything this time?" she asked.

"You said something about God. You know, I do not need to be physically close to you to feel that I am close. I could be on the other side of the country, or a different planet."

"What about a different star or galaxy, or even universe?"

"Even that; anywhere, it does not matter where or how much time might separate us, I will feel this close."

"As close as this?" She pressed herself up against him and kissed him again and hard. Breaking off, she asked, "But what do you mean by that? Do you mean we do not have a future; that there will be a great span of time separating us? You mean I'm going to die?"

Patrick kissed her. He kissed her again, then again. "Don't be silly."

"Will we have a life together?" she asked. "Serious, I'm wondering if we will."

"Of course we will."

Emily thought a moment. "That is what Alessandra says too and she never lies. Alessandra always says what is right and true, doesn't she?"

"My mother can speak to the river, summon the sun, and redirect the moon with the tips of her fingers."

"I like that; it is her, really. Of course, you would know; you are her son."

Emily sat up and swung her feet off the edge of the bed. She stood and stretched, naked. "I feel good; a bit weak, maybe." She placed her hands on her ribs and turned to face him, posing. "I'm a bit thin, though, don't you think?"

"You are perfect, every proportion just right."

She leaned forward, hovering over him. She kissed him, but quickly straightened before he could reach for her. She held his hand, pressing it to her body, between her breasts; she then released it, letting his hand fall away as she shifted to the window.

"I have never noticed how the spring fights to return," she said quietly, peering out through a crack in the curtain. She turned, her hand still holding the curtain open. "It is too dark now, and I can't see them at the moment, but I remember seeing a cluster of crocuses' by the fence yesterday. You know, the black fence with the spears reaching upward leading toward the park? The crocuses poking out through the snow? Life struggling - I know what that's like, don't I?"

She let the curtain fall back into place and returned quickly to the bed, slipping beneath the sheets and into

Patrick's arms. "It is chilly out there, and it's not winter; it is nearly spring. What do you think is going on? I didn't sign up for weather like this!"

"Alessandra called me this morning," Patrick informed her as he turned out the light. He knew he would have all of Emily's attention.

"What did she say?"

"Don't worry, she said – chin up. Smiley face."

"Ha!" Emily laughed. She thought, snuggling in before whispering. "...Thank you for that; I needed that."

EMILY, BEAUTIFUL EMILY

Emily, beautiful Emily, who had been told by Alessandra that "beauty is a light in the heart," slowly stood up from her chair, held onto the windowsill for support, and once again looked out the window. She noticed how the spring fought to return. She had not noticed that before – how it fought and how it struggled. She was noticing a lot more these days, and standing with her forehead pressed against the cold glass, her breath fogging the surface, she absorbed without really seeing the shifting shadows on the wet grass, and the wind lifting the dead leaves too damp to fly from the newly exposed earth. She pushed back from the window but kept looking beyond the glass, noticing how the slope of the bank fell to the sidewalk that led, not in a straight line, but in a sweeping arc to the black, paint-flaked spears opening to the greening park. She smiled when she realized she was seeing all of these things, all at once.

She was alone in her father's house. She didn't like the cold silence but liked the way the sun dropped through the windows onto the hardwood floors reflecting back to fill the room with light.

She recalled how Alessandra had once sat in the cane-backed chair beside her bed, leaning forward, her legs crossed, her elbow on her knee, her chin resting upon the heel of her hand as she smiled and composed her stories of glacial winters, frantic springs, and summers that lasted forever. She remembered how she lay in her bed with her head on the pillow listening, her mind in the world of Alessandra's making, her body safe beneath the coolness of the cotton sheet. Alessandra told her of her perfect world, her Village of the Heart, where we all go, she said, when the day is done, and the night is upon us.

"In dreams, Alessandra?"

"Yes, my love, in dreams."

Their talks were many, every time they were together. There was nothing mechanical between them, nothing formalized. How Emily looked forward to those talks. They sat in her room, Alessandra in the chair next to her bed reaching across to hold her hand, and Emily propped up with a host of pillows. Emily could not get enough of Alessandra's presence. She could not get enough of Alessandra's voice gently moving her through her memories, sweeping her up and floating her down with only her smile and laughter. Alessandra would come every day, not always at the same time, but every day.

Once, Alessandra told her how she felt when she thought of love. Various kinds of love, she explained; traditional love between a man and a woman; the love one feels for a child; a love of life; all kinds of love. She also imagined – evoked was the word she used as she touched the place above her breast beneath which beat her heart – a world with soft warm wind, new grass, and the blue sea washing up on white sand.

She squeezed Alessandra's hand and the pressure was immediately returned. That is what she did when she wanted Alessandra to explain, to add detail, and she always did, the pressure of her hand always returned. On the occasion upon which she was thinking, she had added sun-filled afternoons, crisp autumn mornings, and the way leaves dance in the wind that spill down from the hills to the river. Alessandra had then challenged her to think of such things. She always challenged her. She wanted her to see and feel as well as remember, she said. Emily thought and managed to describe warm summer evenings, crickets and peepers singing beneath the stars, soft rain through the high trees, the sound of the drops falling, slipping along the hanging leaves to the dark ground, absorbed into summer's earth. The scent of the moistened earth mixing with the high fragrance of white and red peonies bent low, grazing the dark grass with their soft petals.

Alessandra gently laughed as she went on and when Emily finished, she offered, *"Ah, that's... that's good,"* her smile slowly widening. She then quieted, reached across, and placed a loose strand of hair that had become undone back behind Emily's ear. "This is how we live forever," she said and kissed her.

Emily looked down at the empty rain-swept street – still no Alessandra. She felt the chill her absence, and the hollow thumping of her beating heart as she waited. The morning her life began, the morning of the present, Emily recalled how Alessandra had turned to her in the light of window and smiled filling the room with eternal beauty and longing. She recalled how she had held Alessandra so tight that Alessandra could barely breathe. She recalled how she had pressed her face against Alessandra's breast, her body racked with sobs, hot tears pouring out – tears of fear; the fear of being left alone. Alessandra had gently pushed her back but held her close. "It is as if you are drowning, my love," she had said. Emily had backed away, hot tears filling her eyes, blinding her, her heart exploding. Alessandra saw the tears and kissed them away.

Quiet then, still: protected, safe.

"If I could make a wish on a star," Emily said later, not looking at Alessandra but out the window into the deepening night.

Alessandra was tucking the sheets close up about her, bending low to kiss her good night.

"What would you wish for, my love?"

"To live with you forever in the Village of the Heart."

"And so you shall, my love; and so you shall."

A SPECIAL, PRISTINE PLACE

Emily floated off the end of the dock surrounded by tossed, silvery water, a white summer sky, pink granite, and dark, weather-bent pines. If she could once again bathe in those waters, would they cure her? Would the purity of the river, filtered through the great forest surrounding it, draw the poison out of her?

"The water is so clear you can see the bottom twenty feet below and see fish halfway up silently meandering through thin strands of weed," she had told Patrick once.

"It sounds wonderful – beautiful."

"It is a special, pristine place."

The river had become a mirror, a surface of quick silver, surrealistically flat, reflecting the thin blue cloudless sky while concealing beneath the singularity of its surface the infinite dark depths below. The integrity of the silence was broken by the sound of a door opening and then slamming shut – and again. A small voice, a child's, broke the returning silence. Small feet pounded on a wooden dock, echoing then falling away. The child, a little girl, stood at the end, tiptoes over the edge, her favorite stuffed toy dangling from one hand. She stood, blonde curls drooping down to her shoulders, head cocked to one side, aware of the immense silence, unsure if she should break it.

Patrick placed his hand on the child's shoulder as he stared out over the river, his expression sad but also oddly content. The little girl pulled on his hand to gain his attention. "Daddy...!" she began but then breaking into a quick succession of sentences, her voice rising and falling, her words skipping along with energy and life lending sense and perspective to the world. Something about the silence, the blue sky, the river, the fish below, and the weeds that weaved in the slow current. Patrick scooped her up. He tossed her in the air and... life ... became... once again... like the moment the bullet pierces the glass, the moment the humming birds' wings can be seen, the moment a drop of rain impacts the smooth waxy-green surface of a leaf then slips broken and splashing onto the dark surface of the pond. Ever so slowly, frame by frame, the child, legs flailing, arms outstretched, flies through the air. Patrick caught her, and as natural as the sun in the sky, she flew upward again; then pirouetting, her hair rising, floating; her smile, her laugh, her eyes shining, her mouth open, catalyzing astonishment to joy, transforming the day, creating meaning where once there was none, changing everything.

"Look at the river, Elizabetta – the river is so clear you can see the bottom twenty feet below and see fish halfway up!"

He set her down carefully, ensuring she remained steady on her feet, and Elizabetta immediately dropped to her knees and leaned out over the edge of the old dock. Reaching further, stretching out, she lay flat and ran her fingers through the water. Lifting her hand, studying it curiously, the river slipped from her fingers to drip, drip, drip only to mysteriously metamorphose into concentric ripples that opened, wider and wider to disappear somewhere beyond the reflecting infinity of the surface.

"The mystery is everywhere. In us, and in everything."

Emily's eyes flew open. There had been a voice, calling. Unfamiliar. She did not know who. She called out,

"Patrick...?" No response. She sat up. Elizabetta stood by the door wearing her favorite bathing suite, a towel slung over her neck, sandals on her feet. She waved and then turned and ran, flying through the screen door into the night, the door slamming shut behind her.

Emily unwound herself from the chair and followed, maintaining a dignified pace, sharp stones and fallen sticks against her bare feet, proceeding along the path, feeling, too, the coolness of the boardwalk in the early damp of the night. Where could that child be, she wondered, concerned Elizabetta might stumble in the dark, trip and fall: small cuts and scratches on her knees and the heels of her hands that would really hurt. The heat of the day had gathered in the earth, held trapped beneath the pines unable to find its way up into the night. The rich scent wrapped itself about Emily, and wrapped itself about Elizabetta, too, Emily knew. She hoped Elizabetta would breathe it in deeply and remember it.

The dock, the old one, twisted and bent by the ice, reached deep into the shadow of the night at the far end of the pine-needle path leading toward the river's dark edge. She could hear Elizabetta step along the boards, pause, and then sit and swing her legs out over the edge. Emily stepped quietly along the boards toward where she knew she would be. The river was a perfect black, a liquid of empty nothingness that absorbed all light except for the stars, the pinpoint images distorted by random ripples that flowed across the perfect surface, the source a pair of feet slowly and silently churning the black water. She stood over the lowered head of her child only just able to make her out beneath the zodiacal glow.

Elizabetta suddenly flung her arm outward. "Mommy,

look!" Emily looked up. She was pointing toward a new comet that had just begun its swing around the sun, Emily knew, knowing only because Patrick had told her that is what it was the previous evening. It hung suspended above the melting horizon with a tail that reached out across the river toward them.

"It is Daddy's diamond star!" Elizabetta cried.

"It is heaven suddenly unleashed," Emily explained softly; "We can only wonder."

Morning came with the inevitable rising of the sun: a perfect timepiece, one that never stops. Every man and woman who has ever lived has watched it rise and set; has watched as, from the predawn to the rising, it commutes night into the promised blue of the day. Fate moving forward; life rising, transforming the river into a scintillating surface of morning light; an unstoppable trajectory, perfectly predictable, mathematically certain; and yet, in all its certainty, in all its predictability, harbouring the unknown, the merciful unknown.

Emily found Elizabetta beneath the crystal-clear surface gazing upward, her golden hair floating about the innocence of her face; her sightless eyes open; her arms outstretched reaching upward. The rest was nightmare – Patrick lifting her body out – laying her on the dock – performing CPR until he collapsed – closing her eyes – howling at the sky.

There was no point in calling 911. Elizabetta Alessandra Marsh was gone, as if she had never existed at all. Patrick picked her limp form up, carried her to the car, and buckled her into her safety seat. She looked to be asleep; soaking wet but asleep. Her were eyes closed, her head lolling to one side, her wet curls beginning to dry as if she had been in the bath. He drove, occasionally glancing at her sleeping form in the rear-view mirror. When would she awaken? At the hospital, he stopped outside the emergency room, stepped around the vehicle, opened the back door, unbuckled her lifeless form, and carried her in.

It was not Elizabetta Patrick carried, it was herself, Emily knew; she had become Elizabetta, and had, perhaps, been Elizabetta all along.

Emily awoke in the room on the top floor of her father's house with her back to Alessandra, Alessandra holding her close. Alessandra's breathing was slow and measured. Alessandra's heart was just there, just there, Emily knew, through the garment she wore.

The sensation of Alessandra lying next to her was an illusion induced by the sedative she took, induced by years of pain, induced by a deadly growth genetically encoded at birth. The Alessandra she imagined did not exist; she was merely a figment of her imagination, her neurosis, and her fear. There is no mind, no spirit, no heart, or soul; nothing is real. Only my body is real, and my body is failing me, Emily thought. I am nothing more than my body.

Or so Emily would say to Patrick if she could, but he had long since been called in yet again.

Emily felt Alessandra lift out of sleep. Emily reached blindly for her hand, and in the almost complete darkness, her fear rising, Emily could feel Alessandra reflexively hold it tightly in her own. Emily wept. She didn't dare open her eyes for fear Alessandra was not real.

Alessandra kissed her hair then held her more tightly still. Turning Emily toward her, she lifted Emily's hand to her lips and kissed her fingers, then held her cold hand against her sleep-warmed cheek, kissing her open palm.

"It was just a dream, my love; just a bad dream – go back to sleep, now; go back to sleep, all will be well in the morning."

EYES OPEN

Emily opened her eyes. She was lying on her back staring at a featureless ceiling. A silhouette crossed her field of view and then disappeared. She tried to follow; the command given but her body failing to move. The silhouette returned. It was a nurse. Black like Bekele. She had kind eyes.

A gush of cold water followed. Her lips were gently salved. "There you go, dear. ...Doctor Marsh just left. He's a good doctor, one of the best I've seen. He cares, he really does, for us all. I must say this: I have watched quite a number of people come into this place, but I must say you are a real fighter. Doctor Marsh says you're dreaming; you dream for days on end. Is that what keeps you going?"

Emily could not follow. It was just a soft, gentle voice. "I was dreaming the color gold, warm sand, and fast-moving streams, crystal, and silver...," she managed to say.

"That sounds beautiful."

Emily found the strength to nod. Her eyes were wide, looking about the hospice room.

"Have you seen...?" she asked.

"The woman that was here?"

"Yes."

"Is she your mother?"

"Yes."

"She is very attractive, isn't she? If I see her again, I'll be sure to tell her you were looking for her and thinking of her. What's her name?"

"Alessandra."

"Alessandra.... I will tell her."

The nurse disappeared. She was gone. The shadows in the room became longer and the chair beside the bed still empty. Emily could hear her own breathing, shallow and laboured as if originating from someone else.

"Emily."

She turned toward his voice. "You're here!"

"I'm right here."

He stood over her, his face in shadow. He held her hand and his lips brushed her cheek. He whispered into her ear; she could feel his lips brushing, moist and warm. He seemed to say, his voice low and melodic, "I have seen a diamond star chased by the blazing sun slip into the heart of the black desert."

Emily began to cry.

"Don't cry – don't."

"I can't help it. I just – I just feel so much!"

"We don't have much time. You might slip away any moment."

"I'm going to die?"

"No, I mean your mind might slip away."

"Stay! Stay! Please stay!"

Patrick leaned forward and kissed her. He lay on the bed beside her and held her close, the soft sound of his breathing in her ear, body to body. She took his hand and placed it on her breast. "I want you to make love to me," she said. "Prove to me I'm real, and you are real." She wept uncontrollably. "I'm just so tired! I'm just so tired!"

"I know."

She could feel the beating of his heart against her.

"This is it, then? This is love?" she asked breathing

into his shoulder.
	"Yes, this is love."
	"Thank God, thank God, thank God."

WHEREVER HER HEART

Emily remembered Alessandra sitting in the cane-backed chair beside the bed, leaning forward, her legs crossed, and her elbow on her knee, her chin resting upon the heel of her hand as she smiled and composed her stories of glacial winters, frantic springs, and summers that lasted forever. Emily recalled how she lay in her bed with her head on the pillow listening, her mind in the world of her making, her body safe beneath the coolness of the cotton sheet. She told her of her perfect world where we all go, she said, when the day is done, and the night is upon us.

On the first days of winter, Alessandra told how those who populate her perfect world would erect a makeshift pavilion on the ice where families could gather to drink hot chocolate by the gallon, chat, exchange pleasantries of the day, or put on skates and launch themselves off the boards onto the unmarked frozen sheet of the river. Men, women, children, young and old, would, more often than not, turn out with skates already lashed to their feet and scarves tightly wound about neck and face, and begin to skate in unison, their arms linked in a long chain across the ultramarine of the ice. The skaters, perilously whirling this way and that, would appear from the upper reaches of the village to be tiny figures in a china shop, infinitely fragile, helplessly ephemeral, the slightest fumble and they would shatter into tiny pieces on the mirrored surface, skittering their tiny lives away across the steel blue to be lost forever. In this strange world, some very few could be found safely crowded around the pavilion warming their hands and feet next to a blazing fire, but most would be on their feet, playing with their destiny, careless of it, completely content, while laughing into the biting wind.

"But the summers! Ah, the summers!" Alessandra explained.

The summers, although short, are pleasant. Just long enough to grow a single crop on the side of the hills that face the sun. Just long and hot enough to enjoy a few months fishing on the river with sun hats pulled down and fishing rods held languidly over the side of an open boat. Just long enough, to enjoy a few brews down by the jetty and to roast cobs of corn behind the school. Long enough to swim in the crystal waters of the river or set out on a day's climb to ascend the almost vertical cliffs of the protective mountains.

"In this place of eternal light," she would say, "the children sweep aside waving strands of wild rice and dive from the banks of the river with their thin bodies slicing, splashless, into the depths of the crystal water. They dive deep, slipping between golden water lilies and mats of aquatic mint, almost forgetting to breathe as they drift in the warm silence between thin stalks of translucent green reaching up the from the darkness into the rippled sun. And from the peak of the highest mountain young men and women, their breathing labored, their bodies aching and tired from the long climb, find their feet, finally, gripping the glacier snow even as the intense sun sears their exposed flesh. With their eyes carefully shaded, they stand close, joined hand in hand, as they gaze down upon their world with the river connecting it.

"Oh yes! I can see it! I can see it!"

"You are standing on the very peak, Emily! You are pushing yourself to your feet; you feel weak, it's been a long climb, there's very little air, and it's cold, so cold, the wind freezes your skin! Now open your eyes! Just open your eyes and look around you! This world is your world!"

"Ha!"

Alessandra laughed as Emily laughed, throwing her head back as Emily did. She cupped Emily's face in her hands and leaned in. "Don't worry, please don't worry, everything will be all right!"

Emily smiled but then began to cry. "If you say so. I hope so."

SOFT PEACE

The angel stepped out ahead, glancing back over her shoulder, and then breaking into a run. Patrick picked up his pace, but he would not run. He had no illusions about what was waiting for him at the far end of the hall. He knew he had time – not much, but enough. The angel was halfway down the corridor and sprinting ahead. Glancing back again, she stopped, turned about, and waited. As he approached, she grasped his arm and held it to her.

"There's not much time!"

Despite his understanding, and despite the months, days, hours, and minutes he had had to prepare for this moment, Patrick's heart slipped as he neared the open door. Unable to enter, he placed his hand against the jamb and leaned against it. The angel waited patiently, still holding his arm. "It's time... time...." Patrick stepped past her into the room. What he saw was not just death but also the nearly dead, with one foot in and one foot out, and far more shocking because of it. He had imagined throwing himself onto his knees beside her, incessantly calling out to her to cut through the fog of her sedative, to let her know how much he loved her; but instead he found himself hesitant, almost afraid, standing more than an arm's length away from the edge of the bed, only reaching out a tentative hand. Steeling himself, he stepped forward. He knew he was about to touch the reality of the woman he loved, and a piece of himself he had no idea existed just a few months before.

The angel leaned in close as he touched the body. "I'm right here beside you," she whispered, her voice matching the solemnity of the room but also warm and light and full of love.

"I know."

The angel seemed surprised. "You can hear me?"

"Yes, I hear you."

"Look at me, then."

The angel was a beautiful young woman with blond hair held in place with a bright barrette, green eyes, and a smile that revealed everything about her of importance.

"That's you lying there; you are the angel," Patrick said.

"No, no;" the angel shook her head, "I am right here!" She reached up and held his face in her hands. "Can you not feel how warm my hands are?"

He withdrew her hands and held them but then turned away, his body heaving as he fought for control, his sorrow racking him.

The bedridden Emily arched her back, twisted in pain, and called out, her voice hoarse, full of fear, drawing Patrick to her side, tearing his heart inside out.

"Patrick! Patrick! Oh God!"

She opened her eyes and found him. Her eyes were startlingly clear and focused: the morphine, Patrick knew. He silently upped the dosage.

"Patrick?" she called out quietly, returned to the present for a moment but quickly dropping away. She reached for him and he moved in close, nearly lying next to her on the bed.

She placed her hand gently on his chest and withdrew it. She held it up. "There's no blood!" she sighed, incredulous, fighting to keep her eyes open, looking for him.

Misunderstanding her, Patrick grasped her hand and kissed her, held her, kissed her. "You just don't see it," he said, "but it's there. I bleed, I bleed; you don't know how I bleed when I see you like this."

Emily again opened her eyes and found him. "I thought you were dead... the knife.... I thought the Afar killed you; slashed your face; stabbed you in the heart. He could have, you know; he could have! He can be trouble."

Patrick attached the syringe to her IV line and added what she needed and what he had planned to give her – it was the end of his career from that moment.

"Do you feel that?" he asked, giving it a moment to take effect. He leaned forward, kissed her again, then whispered against her ear, answering her question. "Do I feel dead?"

"No..."

"I'm not, I'm not... I'm right beside you alive and well!"

Emily began to cry. "We had no time," she cried. "No home, no children; we didn't get very far, did we?"

Patrick kissed her, held her, and kissed her again.

"Farther than the stars, my love."

"There is something I have to tell you."

"And what is that?"

"Something I should have told you over and over again when I knew it was true."

"What is that?"

"If you love someone, you should always tell them; is that not right?"

"Yes, it is."

She said in emphasis, "It is very important to do this; you may never get another chance."

"Yes, that's true."

"You told me that once."

"I...," he hesitated, trying to recall the moment. "Yes. Yes, I remember."

"You have to know I love you, then," she whispered, her eyes closing, her body falling.

Patrick quickly responded, matching her words just as she said them, "You have to know I love you, then..." and felt a sudden weight lift and fly away just as it raised a smile on her hollowed face. She was asleep. He knew she was asleep. He carefully removed her intravenous.

"This is my love," Patrick announced to no one other than himself in the room. "This is she." He reached down and lifted her from the bed. "I know a place by a river...," he said and shifted the feather-lightness of her in his arms.

He carried Emily past the nurse's station, lifting the duty nurse to her feet, sending her around the counter to follow. The elevator doors opened. "No! No! Doctor Marsh, stop!" Shutting silently, the floor was already selected. The nurse, falling into speechless wonderment, reached to touch Emily's cheek as if to touch the holy, the sacred. "Doctor Marsh... I don't think..." She caressed the lines of Emily's face, following the lines, her wonder and amazement complete, joining with Patrick. "I think she is gone...," she said.

The door opened, and Patrick led the procession of three through Admissions, past X-ray, Ultra-Sound and Security, with no one stopping them but with every witness dropping what they were doing and following in a parade of wondrous silence. The impossible and sacred was before them. Every man, woman, and child could recognize it.

The great glass door leading to the outside hushed

open and the assembly passed through, stepping as a single body into a world of sunshine, open sky, and wonder. A large part of the hospital staff had gathered – nurses, doctors, paramedics, firefighters, cleaning staff, gardeners, passersby, a priest come to offer last rites to a soul waiting in some other dying room. Although the people remained silent, the sounds of the day were all about them: birdsong, traffic noise, a far-off conversation. An errant wind lifted and shook a single towering oak spread out above them. It cascaded along its branches and fell through onto the garden kicking up stray leaves, turning the red, yellow, and white flowerbeds inside out, returning them whole as it passed. Even though the leaves had not yet started to turn, even though it was unusually warm for that time of year, fall was coming, and then winter, and then, again, spring. Everyone felt this. Everyone felt how the ancient sky of blue embraced ephemeral life below. Everyone understood how the sun, giving color and warmth, immortalized them all, all life. They knew why they stood there within this perfect day: Emily carried in the arms of her lover, sunlight falling through the high branches, and she asleep in soft peace

ALESSANDRA

AS MANY TIMES AS NEEDED

Alessandra reached out to Emily who accepted her hands, one in each of her own. With Alessandra's help, she stood up out of her chair allowing the quilt to fall from her shoulders. She felt exposed without the protective covering, but she could feel Alessandra's strength pouring into her to compensate. The source was from where their flesh made contact. It coursed up through her arms and up into the middle of her, filling her. Emily glanced up and was again surprised by the singular nature of the woman: her eyes, her face, the grace of her body, her energy, her power, her beauty.

Alessandra placed an arm around her, set her hand on the small of her back, and carefully turned her to face the length of the porch.

"Are you okay, dear?"

Emily nodded. Their arms were crossed as they faced forward and took the first steps, as if they were dancing or embracing.

"One step at a time, one step at a time...," Alessandra suggested softly, the rhythm of her body and voice smoothing the lurching struggle of Emily's first steps.

"...You are stronger today."

"I feel better, I do...."

Emily forced one foot ahead of the other. "Am I cured?"

"Your body is cured; now all we have to do is work on the rest of you."

Emily nodded her understanding.

"What is this place?" she asked.

"You don't recognize it?"

"Yes.... I think so...."

"Our home, and now your home too."

They achieved the end and Alessandra turned her so they could walk it once more.

"But where is this place?"

"We live in the mountains, beside a river," Alessandra explained quietly. Emily could feel her smiling. "Surely you have heard of it?"

"A special, pristine place?"

Alessandra, turning to her, her eyes and smile following her movement across the porch, her affection and kindness as strong as the force coursing through her, quietly laughed. The sound was rich like the sunshine beyond the porch, full of life like the patchwork of green that seemed to dance in the distance.

"Just so."

The color of life, the scent of life, reached for Emily, drawing her out, lifting her feet, setting them on the boards, promising her that one day soon she would be running their length, jumping off the top step to the cobbled path and through the open picket gate in a full run toward the river.

"Where is Patrick?"

"Patrick won't be back until winter comes again and when you are better, more yourself, dear. He's not happy about it, but there you go. No communication until you are feeling better; those are the rules – my rules, by the way, and not his. He has some explaining to do, to say nothing of graduating, which I insist on. First things first, I'm afraid."

"He's not here?" Emily asked again, still not believing.

"No, I'm afraid not, dear."

"Can I talk to him?"

"No, I'm afraid not."

"Why not?"

Alessandra hesitated then said, "Because before you do – and you will, you will, darling – you need to be more yourself." Alessandra leaned forward and gently placed her hand over Emily's heart. "Let's work on this; let it be all of Emily, and strong first, okay?"

Emily slowly nodded her understanding. She looked out over the green field dotted with red and gold poppies. They seemed to shift, turn to track the sun. "I remember landing on the ice," Emily said as Alessandra sat her gently into the cane-back chair at the end of the porch. "The tremendous noise, whirling of blades, snow flying everywhere; cold air, freezing cold air; blue sky above. Helmeted men jumping onto the ice. The deafening noise stopped, and then I saw you and I knew everything would be okay."

"Yes, that's right."

"I saw a tall black man; was that Bekele?"

"He was, indeed."

"He was not wearing a helmet or one of those orange suits, but he had headphones on, and of course a woollen toque. Where is he now?"

"He went back almost immediately. First flight out which was approximately ten minutes later. We barely had time to say hello never mind goodbye. He did manage to pay a very short but very special visit while he was here, which I had previously arranged. He dropped everything, risked everything, for his brother because that is what brothers do. I am very proud of him. You might wonder what sisters would do under similar circumstances; something similar but not like that, I would think; not that life and death commitment intertwined with fate that brothers seem to share – some brothers, that is."

Emily smiled and then nodded, and then said what she cared about most. "But what I really want to know is why Patrick wasn't on the chopper."

"Not part of the plan, I'm afraid. Someone had to remain behind to answer the rather long list of questions that would inevitably be raised. But you had excellent medical attention. We ensured you were unconscious for most of the flight. It was Patrick's idea, and a good one; you didn't complain one bit."

Emily tipped her head back, chin up, to take in all of Alessandra. "You are just as I imagined you."

Alessandra cupped Emily's face in her free hand. "Not this old and haggard, surely?" She quietly laughed so as not to disturb the greater morning beyond the porch.

Alessandra helped Emily back onto her feet, taking her hands, and drawing her up.

"One more time along the boards?" she suggested.

"And one more time after that," Emily agreed.

Alessandra turned her to face once again the length of the porch, threading her arm through Emily's.

"As many times as needed, my love; as many times as needed."

HEART,
BRITISH COLUMBIA

THE VILLAGE

In all of time, in all that there is stretched between now and yesterday, exists the village of Heart, British Columbia. It is a fantastical place, held by time, protected from fate, forever youthful. It flourishes between cloud-enshrouded mountains and a starkly still river that sweeps into existence from behind the foot-lands and then disappears into the mountains and cloud as it cuts in a tight arc past a small village made of white-washed homes. The homes, neat and orderly, are tightly clustered along a road that drops from the airless heights then splits left and right and follows the bank of the river. There is a single church with a spire that reaches up higher than any other dwelling; there is a general store with a sign proudly saying, "General Store," and a school with its back to the mountains and its feet almost in the dark waters. There is a library, a town hall, firehall, and a garage with an overhead sign weathered to near invisibility which says simply, "Garage."

Springs in Heart, British Columbia are impossible. Life explodes from the earth fully born in flower and scent. As the villager's watch, opened-mouthed, always astounded, the snow disappears, cascading in mad torrents of suddenly released water down the slopes into the river. Crocuses carpet the ground and daffodils explode, transforming their fields of sudden green into instant seas of flowing silver and gold. All around them red and white tulips thrust themselves up through the dark earth, twisting, cavorting, reaching up for the light. The lilacs... the lilacs fill the warm moist air with their heavy fragrance mixed with the scent of the freshly turned earth and falling apple blossoms.

Even in the coldest winter days, villagers will turn to one another and say, *"I think I might be gettin' a whiff of lilac...!"* *"Uhmmm... I think so too...!"* And then some wit would add, *"Spring is sprung, the lilac's come...!"* and would look around in feigned panic for something solid to stand on.

Summers, although short, are pleasant, just long enough to grow a single crop on the side of the hills that face the sun. Just long and hot enough to enjoy a few months fishing on the river with sun hats pulled low and fishing rods held languidly over the side of an open boat; just long enough to enjoy a few brews down by the jetty or roasting corn behind the school. Long enough to swim in the crystal waters of the river or set out on a day's climb to ascend the almost vertical cliffs of the protective mountains.

In this village of sacred light, the children sweep aside waving strands of wild rice, and dive from the banks of the river with their thin bodies slicing, splash-less, into the depths of the crystal water. They dive deep, slipping between rafts of yellow and white water-lilies and mats of aquatic mint, almost forgetting to breathe as they drift in the warm silence between thin stalks of translucent green reaching up from the darkness into the rippled sun. And from the peak of the highest mountain, young men and women, their breathing labored, their bodies aching and tired from the long climb, find their feet, finally, gripping the glacier snow even as the intense sun sears their exposed flesh. With their eyes carefully shaded, they stand close, joined hand in hand as they gaze down upon their world with the river connecting it. In the hollow silence, with only the secretive wind in their ears, they find their homes nestled amidst all the immensity, placed likes toys along the thin ribbon of road, while imagining how it would be to stand on their porch and look upward to where they currently stood, marvelling at it all, their tears freezing to their cheeks.

Then there are the winters. It is not unusual to have more than forty feet of snow drifting up against the sides of the homes, and in some cases completely burying the roof making them often indistinguishable from the mountain slopes leading to the banks of the river. From the very first day of winter, it is quite common to have individual homes linked by tunnels of snow and ice that twist from door to door, the tunnels propped up by stalactites, sub-glacial signposts, to mark the way. On days that people farther south could not possibly imagine, villagers of all ages ski from their barely exposed and jagged rooftops, swooshing down the slope that leads to the wind-swept sheet of blue steel that has become the river.

By the first few days of winter, the village erects a makeshift pavilion on the ice where families gather to put on skates and warm themselves beside the stove or drink hot chocolate by the bucket full. The short winter days create a festival mood with the entire village – men, women, and children, young and old – turning out with skates on and scarves tightly wound about neck and face. They skate as a single body, their arms linked in a long chain across the ultramarine of the ice.

It gets cold, very cold, and it feels even colder with the wind chill. By January, it is cold enough to seize the evaporating coils that make up the still behind the fire hall, often encasing the precious high-proof liquid in an almost – that is almost – impenetrable shroud of ice. Even so, the villagers brave the numbing conditions every day. With the long hours of winter stretching ahead, they frolic in the frozen chill with rosy cheeks, their breath like hot clouds of pressurized steam rising and then trailing behind them.

During one of the coldest winters anyone could remember, and with four or five times more snow that anyone knew possible, Patrick managed to find his way home. His truck was heard before it could be seen slowly appearing from behind the tortured ridges of snow, magically coalescing like some phantom out of the haunted and impenetrable mist that always clings to the mountain pass. He pulled up in front of his Alessandra's home; his home, too, by definition, and since plowing had long since been abandoned, parked immediately opposite the second-floor window that led to what would become his bedroom, at least for a short while.

He pushed open the truck door, pulling up his collar and hood. He could hear music from the pavilion and laughter floating in the air, carried by the wind. His face, once solemn and tired, thoughtful with even a shrift of trepidation, shifted then coalesced into an indefinable shape: happiness and sadness, anticipation and dread. He braced himself, throwing back the hood of his coat, purposely turning his face into the cold wind to clear his mind.

Patrick, standing beside his 4x4, faced the bedroom window there was so much snow. Conveniently unlocked, he drew it up. He backed himself in by sitting on the sill then ducking low and twisting about. Inside, feet on the wooden floor, he removed one boot quickly followed by the other then jumped up and shut the window to preserve what little heat remained in the room. He threw his bag on his old bed made up as if Alessandra had been expecting him – he had not told her he was coming; not today anyway – then lingered in the familiarity of the bedroom, turning slowly about, surprised and pleased by what he saw. He glanced at his unnaturally uncluttered desk he used to sit at and study, Bekele with his headphones on listening to the music he loved so much, and then climbed up onto his old bed and ran his fingers along the headboard, quickly finding the carved characters that spelled his name. He smiled, shaking his head, amazed, and climbed off the bed, and an old memory flashed. He turned to the door looking for but of course not finding the pencil marks that would start less than three feet above the wooden floor and ending just short of six.

"The taller you get, the better the view; the better the view, the more you see...," Francesco – or shall we say Francis – had said with every mark. Patrick smiled. Francesco, dead now but still alive.

He paced the room, exploring the desk drawers, the empty dresser, beneath the bed noting the dustless floor immaculately swept clean by Alessandra. Smiling openly now, he opened the bedroom door and called down the stairs toward the light at the bottom, "Hey!" He listened through the hesitant silence, quickly rewarded by the anticipated rattling of dishes, the running of water, a chair pushed back, and an unmistakable voice calling up the stairs, "Patrick! Is that you?" followed by the sound of slipper-clad feet dancing hurriedly across the kitchen floor toward the landing at the bottom of the stairs. "You moved all of our stuff here!" he shouted down the stairs. "Why did you do that? It must have cost a fortune!"

The reunion of mother and son occurred on the bottom step with Patrick wrapping his arms about Alessandra's slim shoulders and giving her a hug that lasted a full wordless minute. His throat tightened on his hug's return. In control again, he stepped back and held at arm's length the woman who could speak to the river, summon the sun, and redirect the moon with the tips of her fingers.

"Here is what I want, Patrick – I won't fool with you; I want you to stay. This is your home now too, yours and Emily's. You do not have to answer right away, take your time. There are a few things you must learn first and know, especially about Emily." Alessandra stepped back, taking in all of him, wiping at her happy tears. "You will have lots of questions, I know, and I will do my best to answer them in time. I have a whole script prepared. More stories – I know how much you used to like my stories. Not winter, this time, but people." She smiled again and stepped in close, hugged him, kissed Patrick's cheek, and then whispered in his ear. "Thank God you are here!" Alessandra then laughed, throwing her head back as Patrick spun her through the air and laughed with her, overjoyed to be home again after such a long drought.

AN INSTANCE OF TIME

Our world is always, Alessandra once explained, at that instant of time when the first breath of life opens the lips and throws back the head; the instant when atoms collide and shower the universe with something new.

Days, weeks, months, years later – time is irrelevant in Heart, British Columbia – found Patrick anticipating yet another inhumanly cold morning with its surrealistically clear sky, and sunlight so intense it burned exposed flesh to a crisp and stabbed unprotected eyes into sightless orbs. He opened his bedroom window and inhaled the cold air, held it to warm it, then slowly exhaled to see the anticipated column of white steam rise up and condense to crystals of ice.

The evening before he and Alessandra had sat for hours close to the warmth of the stove sipping hot chocolate as they laughed and wandered through shared memories.

With the stove door open and the coals dancing red and white, Alessandra casually said, "Francis is in the boathouse. He'll be there until spring." She shoved in a piece of wood and added, "Emily... Emily will show you."

"Emily?"

"Emily – surely you have heard of her; she is about this high, blonde hair, green eyes?"

"Ah, yes; *that* Emily!"

Francis in the boathouse – that didn't make sense; Patrick ignored it, consumed as he was about seeing Emily again; it had been almost a year.

Alessandra kicked the stove door shut before falling

back into her chair. "Phew! That's hot! So.... So, now you are out of prison," she stated, sitting back and settling, her smile and the way she settled implying she was preparing for a long conversation and perhaps he should too. "I am so very proud of you, Patrick; we all are," she added. "You have done so much, but now you are here with us again, and that is the best of things, isn't it?"

"I did have a lot of explaining to do but I was never incarcerated. And what do you mean by 'again'?"

"You have graduated, too, which is an absolutely wonderful accomplishment! Another achievement for which we are very proud of you, all of us."

"Who is all of us, exactly?"

"All of us, who do you think?"

He almost said, 'Other than the three, I am a solitary man.' He said instead, "Dr. Ansari and the entire staff came to my defence; I am still moved, too, to the degree to which they put their reputations on the line for me."

"It is true that there were hundreds involved. I am proud of them all, but you especially; and Bekele, too, of course."

"Yes, Bekele was brilliant; but I am not the only who is curious about how you managed it all: what strings you must have pulled. You must walk in high places, Alessandra."

Alessandra smiled and primed just a little. "Well, it is true, I did enjoy myself. But I am sorry I cannot offer an explanation; someday I will, but not at this time. I hope you understand."

"I understand – to a point. I admit I am curious but not as curious as those demanding to know. Heads have already rolled."

"No doubt. But you should know that all those involved were offered a fair bargain, that much at least I will tell you."

"Such as?"

"Well, let's see... How about guaranteed good health until they die?"

Patrick jolted with surprise quickly shifting to incredulity. "You are not capable of offering that, no one is."

"Well, they all did their part, didn't they? Something must have motivated them, other than knowing deep down that it was the right thing to do."

"I cannot imagine how that could be... human nature. When I go back, I'm sure to be hauled up on the carpet."

"Don't go back."

"They can find me here; extradite me from the heart of one of their provinces."

"I don't think so, and sarcasm does not become you."

Patrick sighed. He ran his hand through his hair. "You know," he said, giving up for the moment, "I still sometimes wonder why I went through all the training to be, first a medical doctor, and then a neurologist. For all my knowledge, for all I can do, it does not seem nearly enough."

"Is your concern chiefly that you could not save Emily, but I could, and have?"

"That pretty much sums it up."

"We can only do what we can do, Patrick: all of us, myself included. It was nothing; nothing, really – I will explain, I will, and I know you want to know, but what you just said bothers me. You are currently one of the best trained neurologists in the world and yet you wonder if it was all worth it? What a thing to say! Of course, it was worth it! Do you recall why you elected to go medical school in the first place? I remember it like yesterday if you do not."

Sunday morning after church. Rome. The three of them sitting on stone benches facing one another in the heart of their private *giardino* beneath the trellised roses, listening to the trickling water while trying to escape the heat. Francisco holding up a letter written by Patrick addressed to the Applications Committee of King's College, London. "So this is it, is it? You worked hard on it. Do you want me to read it?" Patrick nodded. "I am privileged you should ask me. I am not the most careful reader, or the most astute in grammar or turn of phrase; I can barely read English without moving my lips. Now, if this were in Italian...." Alessandra: "Do not be silly, Francis! Please read it aloud." "Hmmm... yes;" he read aloud: "why I want to be a medical doctor.... Well....," Francesco silently read it through. He read through twice, flipping the page each time. Finished, he looked up at Patrick and read the letter aloud from memory.

"I have thought long and hard about what my life means, and have concluded that , if I can do just one good thing, lift one small life out of just one of the many hells that afflict us, then I believe I can, perhaps, accomplish something meaningful. I believe this with all my heart."

Francesco finished, nodding slowly. "It is perfect. Don't change a word. Well done. Mail it today. I will take it to the post office myself."

"Where did that sentiment go, I wonder?" Alessandra asked sitting across him, the stove ticking along.

Patrick would not answer. He realized it had not gone

anywhere. He had misspoken. It had become temporarily buried and he did not know why. He admitted as much.

Alessandra added, "The *Danakil* is a desert, Patrick; one of the hottest, driest, and most lifeless places on Earth, and you brought it here with you. You have been separated from Emily for almost exactly one year, and the Danakil has reared up again in you. I have a way of removing it, if you let me."

"How is that?"

"It is simple, really – a kiss from a very much changed girl who loves you still. That and a few boring but informative hours listening to what I have to say, and the rain will once again quench the parched earth and the garden will bloom as it used to."

"That is ridiculous!"

"Nope, just a few stories; the kiss comes later – if Emily decides to do so, and she might decide not to; you know what she's like. I did mention, at least I inferred, there are no guarantees here. You know, thinking about it, I might have been a little over the top: parched earth, and all that, but you know what I mean."

"I am too old for stories."

"No, you are not! Without a little background on what this place is and who I am, who Emily has now become, and who are, too, what you are about to face as you climb out your bedroom tomorrow morning might otherwise be a bit of a shock; for you, not for Emily, and certainly not for the village.... Do not roll your eyes, it is unbecoming of you – sorry for a being your mother. Are you ready? It's nice, don't worry. Just a few stories; you used to like them! They are a bit of fun."

Patrick buried his face into his hands and shook his

head. He could not win.

"Fine, then, here it goes: hold onto your hat!" She took a deep breath and began in her storytelling voice. "You see, Abigale Mary Marsh was my mother. Pappy John Smith was my father – Pappy stood for Clarence, by the way; no one wanted to call him Clarence, as you might understand. Abigale and Pappy were never married, not in a church but married in their hearts, you know – married in their heart is a famous phrase around here; frankly, they eloped. No big deal around here either. Your father and I pretty much did the same thing, but, in our case, we left the village, headed out into the wild blue, as is said, but inevitably to return as we all do eventually."

"I have an extended family," Patrick asked, incredulous. It might not be true, he reminded himself; it might only be part of the story not meant to be taken literally.

"Yes – or, I should say, had; they are all dead now; gone to the *Nappin' Place* long ago: better part of spring, and all that."

Alessandra pressed on. "And so, on one of the hottest days of August, my mother ran down to the jetty and awakened my father from the deepest of slumbers. He was sitting in his old Peterborough with his old friend Fred McHarg, their lines over the edge, stripped of the bait. They were both sound asleep."

"A Peterborough is a boat, by the way; a cedar strip, sixteen feet long with wooden seats thwart to thwart. It comes with oars and an outboard motor and is usually painted with a red stripe from bow to stern, the remainder varnished. The old boat still floats – it's a bit leaky. It is currently upside down by the boat house beneath the snow. You and Emily can take it out in the spring, if you like."

"And why...? I mean, what is all this about? Is this an allegory of some sort? If so, I...."

"A gentle bump is what this is about, so bear with me."

"A gentle bump?"

"A gentle bump – please allow me to continue. A gentle bump awakened Pappy and Fred." Alessandra mimicked the old-timers. She was good at it. "'What da?' says Fred, sitting bolt upright and giving his friend a swift kick. Pappy, wide awake, removed his marble eye, rubbed it on his sleeve, then returned it.

"'Are you seein' what I'm seein', Freddy, ol boy?' he says.

"'I dunno...'

"'Better pick 'er up, there, Freddy,' Pappy says, his pipe firmly in place as was his eye. Fred nodded, nervously wiping his hands on his trousers before reaching over the gunwale. He picked up the little package that had gathered their rapt attention and held it close as Pappy started up the 'Rude and slowly turned the Peterborough around."

She returned to her normal voice. "By the way, Patrick, 'Rude' is the name and manufacturer of the outboard motor – in this case a 1962 Evinrude; single cylinder, ten horsepower. It nearly always starts on the first pull – if there's gas in the tank, that is, and you have the choke on. You do have a lot to learn, Patrick, if you plan on staying with us for any length of time, and I hope you do, I really do."

"I'm too old for these stories."

Alessandra laughed. "You said that already, and, no, you are not! Anyway, once alongside the jetty, Fred lifted the little package up – he surely knew what it was by then – to three hundred pairs of welcoming arms. You see – and this is the important part so pay attention – the entire village had assembled – call it community spirit – and as my mother lifted the covering to reveal what was hidden beneath, they all gasped in wonder while my mother cried over and over, *'My baby! My baby!'"*

"Uh-huh."

"That was me; I was the baby."

"I got that."

"But what you do not understand, or could possibly appreciate, my son, or even imagine, perhaps, is the sound of the village cheering. Their cheers resounded along the river, up the slopes to ring in the mountains, coloring the sun a deeper gold, the sky a more magnificent blue. And as the village swept the new mother and child into their loving embrace, the trees danced, and the blue water of the river began to ripple with delight!"

"Uh-huh...A bit of an exaggeration there." Patrick was unsure what the point was, or even if there was a point. But perhaps that was the point, he thought, and, despite himself, he laughed.

Alessandra, catching his improved humor, laughed with him. "I like that; you are laughing! I know it sounds a bit much, but it is entirely true, at least the essentials are. It was how I was delivered to the world. Your delivery was much more mundane I have to tell you."

"Okay."

"I was delivered by the river."

"So I gathered."

"No big deal, I suppose."

"Not really."

"Don't make fun."

"I'm not."

"I only exaggerated where needed for the sake of the telling."

"I am sure that is true - but I am sorry I missed them all, if, indeed, they are not part of the exaggeration: Abigale and Pappy, my grandmother and grandfather, and all the others. You might have to tell the story again because I can't quite recall all their names: it is quite a list. When did they pass on?"

"Well before your time, about three hundred years ago," Alessandra offered without flinching. "I have inherited some things from the river, you should know, too. The list is short – or long, depending how you parse it out."

Patrick laughed again, feeling light-headed and more than just a little incredulous. "Keep going then, don't stop now! I want to know all about them."

"We do have all night, don't we?" his mother said, brushing her hair back with her hand, and smiling, relieved that Patrick wanted to continue.

"We do indeed - and don't leave any of the good parts out," Patrick suggested with a smile, motioning Alessandra to continue.

"Good parts? Oh, yes, I see! Don't worry, I won't."

I AM NOT MY BODY

With the world newly born, fresh and bright and insanely cold, Patrick climbed the stairs, threw open his bedroom window, brushed back the snow, and climbed out into the new world. He spilled out headfirst. He laughed, groaned, and quickly removed a glove to brush away the stinging ice. Quickly replacing his glove – he did not want to lose any fingers – he pushed himself up onto his knees and squinted against the brilliant glare down toward the reflecting ribbon of the river.

The skaters, perilously whirling this way and that, appeared as tiny figures in a china shop, infinitely fragile, helplessly ephemeral; the slightest fumble and they would shatter into tiny pieces on the hard surface, skittering their tiny lives away across the steel blue to be lost forever. Some were safely crowded around the pavilion warming their hands and feet before a blazing fire, but most were on their feet playing with their destiny, careless of it, completely content.

Patrick strapped on his skis, goggles in place, pole-straps tight about his wrists, his body loose and ready, and then threw himself into the void. He followed the contour of the steeply pitched roof, jumped the street, and then fell vertically to the river. He was flying, in free fall, and hit the ice with his body in a low crouch, his scarf and parka pressed back, his eyes streaming with tears. He clattered over the ice, his skis bouncing and rattling, dangerously unstable, and finally came to a stop halfway across the river. He tilted back his head and shouted – lifting his poles, jumping clear, his skis slapping down, spinning about, opening his arms to embrace the river, the banks of snow, the village and mountains.

"Ha!"

Thousands of times he had done this, and for thousands of times it was always different but wonderfully the same – or so it felt, and from what Alessandra had told him the previous evening, feeling that way may not be all that unusual; that is, if a feeling can be inherited.

Patrick kicked off his skis and yanked on his cold-stiffened skates. Quiet now, the full silence of a winter morning settling upon him, able now to hear the most the silent of things, he spotted a solitary figure skating out from the pavilion, and from the reach of her legs and the twist of her arms he knew it was Emily.

He had been looking forward to their impending reunion, and not looking forward to it at the same time. Almost a year – no, as of today, exactly a year.

Emily shot past him, her doppler-shifted laugh *"Haaaaaaaah!"* preceding her, the unexpected shockwave that followed nearly knocking him off his feet. She turned in a wide arc back toward him and seconds later Patrick found himself showered by a mountainside of crystalline ice, the tiny particles penetrating even the tiniest pinhole of his parka. He wiped at his face to clear his eyes as a warm hand reached into his collar to extract an especially uncomfortable wedge.

"Better?"

First words.

With only her eyes showing above her scarf, and despite her toque, there was no doubt at all about the identity of the skater. She tore off her hat and scarf, and Emily, beautiful Emily, her green eyes turning to blue to match the sky behind her, her face flushed, her smile explosive, slowly bowed. *"Emily Martina Portinari at your service!"* Straightening, there she was, all of her, all at once, her blonde hair pulled back and tied behind her ears, held in place by a shining diamond barrette that flashed in the winter sun.

"I like your barrette."

"Thank you!"

Second words.

"They are real diamonds, you know." She nearly laughed saying so. "It is good to see you!" she also said. She radiated like the sun.

"It is you."

"Of course, it's me! And...?"

"I had forgotten you could skate."

"Of course, I can skate! Is that all you have to say?"

"I missed you."

She stepped in close. "Oh! Well, okay, that's good," she said and smiled. She abruptly recovered and reached for his arm. "Let's go!"

Patrick's heart lifted, floated, as they stepped out in synchronization across the ice with her arm through his.

He managed, stammering, as they skated across the ultramarine ice harder than steel, "So, I hear you are brand new."

"Yep, brand new."

"Something I could not do...."

She cut him off. "Never mind that! Come on!" She pulled him along. *"Come, come, come, come...!* I saw you ski down from Alessandra's house – not bad!"

They skated, toy figures stretching into a brilliant sun, the ice a mirror.

"I have something to show you," she said lightly. "I am afraid that I am obliged to; Alessandra said the what, the where, the who, and the when, and I am her dutiful slave. Who am I but to obey?"

"Do you obey my mother in all things?"

"Do you?"

Patrick turned to catch her expression. Emily had tipped her head back and closed her eyes turning to face the sun, then turning back to smile. Whatever image was in her mind she kept it to herself.

"You and Alessandra had a long chat last night," she said returning to him.

"Yes, we did. The fact I apparently have an extended family living here, or at one time having lived here, seemed to be her main point. A few more things, too, that I am not so certain are meant to be taken literally. They may have been allegorical. I am still trying to absorb it all."

"Well, that's good. And here you are once again, loved by everyone for all time."

He wondered what she meant.

They skated on.

"...And just to be clear," she added, looking beyond to the mountains and the wisps of cloud catching the peaks, "This is now my home and I'm not leaving it anytime soon." She caught his eye and admitted with a smile, "...Well, except for the odd vacation here and there, which doesn't count." She threw her head back but didn't laugh; her widening smile said what she felt.

Patrick nodded, shaking his head up and down and then from side to side, not sure what to say. "Good," he finally managed.

Emily continued to smile. "Good is good, I guess!" She

laughed then.

They skated up to the pavilion, and once the overflowing mugs of hot chocolate already prepared for them were handed over, the villagers went about self-consciously ignoring them, only a handful out of two dozen or more glancing at Emily, catching her eye, smiling, but then quickly looking away to continue with their gossip.

A young girl, blue toque, green scarf wrapped around her face with only her eyes showing; white snowsuit, red woollen mittens to match her toque; blond hair like Emily's, skated past them then slowly returned, skating in a wide arc back toward them, occasionally lifting her scarf to sip at her chocolate, glancing at Emily and smiling, glancing curiously at Patrick then skating past. She repeated the motion, and again before she finally stopped before them.

"We all know who you are," she said facing Emily but nonetheless addressing Patrick, and with the spell broken she skated away as, one by one the villagers approached, and one by one welcomed Patrick, shaking his hand, each removing his or her glove first, Patrick having already removed his. "Welcome back, Paddy, ol' boy!" they each said in turn. "Welcome back, sweetie!" "You have been gone a long while; your life up to this point!" some wit added to a chorus of laughter. "Let's hope you stick around a little longer this time." An avalanche followed. "Welcome back – you are a good-looking lad; you look like your mother!"

"Big dance tonight," the young girl announced returning to their side when the rounds had been made. She faced Patrick and bowed. Straightening, she said, "I would give you my card except I seem to have forgotten it." Another bout of heady laughter at Patrick's expense. She curtsied prettily, turning to acknowledge those who had applauded with a smile and another bow. Turning back, she removed her scarf then her toque. She was eleven or twelve and exceptionally pretty. "But may I have first dibs?"

"Of course, I would be honored."

The girl bowed and curtsied to another uproar of hilarity.

Emily laughed. "That's Abigale; the current version of your late grandmother. She is a lot of fun, but a handful. In a good way." She indicated the cup in his hand. "Finished?"

Patrick nodded and then drained it. The villagers had retreated a respectful distance, their backs turned to them; the odd one – the young blue-toque, red-mittened, blue-eyed girl otherwise known as Abigale most notably – glancing back occasionally: Abigale twice, maybe three times more.

"You are quite a hit."

"They seem an interesting lot, if not a bit odd. They laugh at nothing."

Emily began to explain but then throwing her gloved hands in the air gave up. "It is far better to laugh than cry," she said instead.

They jumped off the pavilion onto the ice, gliding, the pristine cold, encompassing, and pure.

Patrick asked, "Where did you say we were going?"

"I didn't – but you probably know; Alessandra said she told you. You may not have picked up on it, but she did tell you."

Their presumed destination remained barely discernible, its shape and form almost lost against the rising bank of snow and gathering darkness forming at the edge of the mirror of ice. Night had fallen, the stars in riot, the sky a flood of magical shifting color, the sacred silence broken only by the cracking of the ice and the sound of their steel blades cutting into the glass surface.

They stepped up onto the snow-covered boards, opened the heavy door. It was colder inside than out, and completely dark without a sliver of light and formidably quiet. Emily threw a switch and a powerful lamp simulating the sun snapped to life. The glare threw Patrick's hands up to protect his eyes. He gradually lowered them: hay on the worn floor, blocks of cut ice stacked in the corner, and as his vision recovered further, the vision of Francesco sitting upright in an open boat, the proverbial Peterborough, holding an unstrung fishing pole in one hand and a bottle of beer complete with a column of frozen froth overflowing the narrow neck in the other. He stepped in closer; here was the man who had once lifted him onto his shoulders to carry him over fields of gold; here was his father; here is Francesco, he thought, still unable to react.

"He has been like this for some time now, more than two years," Emily quietly explained from behind him.

"Bekele?"

"He was here just long enough to see. He promised not to tell you, and from your expression I can see he did not."

There was a contusion on his forehead, a bandage pasted across it.

"He hit his head?"

"Yes, on the ice, barrel jumping – the main cause of

death for men, and women, too, over the age of fifteen."

Patrick reached up to touch his father's face, feeling the frozen stubble, the wax-like quality of the skin. "He's gone," he said, incredulous, overwhelmed.

Emily whispered, "But if I were gone, dead, less than half of who I am – missing an arm or a leg – would you not still love me?"

She stood close behind him; he could feel her radiated warmth and detect the sweet fragrant scent of her like spring.

"Alessandra said if I kissed you, the world would change," she said and reached around him and gently pecked his lips. She leaned in so their foreheads touched. "I am not my body, and I am my body," she said and kissed him lightly again.

She stepped back wiping at her eyes. "That's it, for now.... I will be just outside."

She waited by the boathouse door, an outline of a parka-ed figure against the backdrop of snow, ice, and zodiacal light. The artificial sun dimmed then went out entirely. The boathouse door opened and then closed. The latch fell into place. When he was close, she took his hand and drew him to her.

"I see... I see...," she said looking up at the stars, struggling to explain. Patrick could see her clearly, illuminated only by the light of the stars cast like a host of diamonds above them. "I see further than the stars sometimes," she said.

They stepped off the boards onto the infinite sheet of ice that made up the river and skated out, arm in arm, steel on steel, beneath the canopy of heaven. The river reached out beneath them, the stars insane above their heads. They danced. She twirled beneath his raised arm then fell back into his arms. They looked upward, her head against his shoulder. She turned in his arms and Patrick kissed Emily for the first time, and the ice cracked. The night, time, the stars in heaven, the world stretching about them, changed at that moment; from that moment forward, nothing would ever be the same, not for them, not ever.

OTHER STORIES

ABIGALE AND PAPPY

It could not be said that Pappy was one of the originals, but it could be said he was one of the oldest – used to be one of the oldest, that is – residents of the village. His memory – used to – stretch back further than anyone's.

"The world was different then," he'd say. "I can't believe the changes that have occurred since I squibbled out into the world, smokin' me pipe, they says; right from the beginn', they says – and it didn't kill me neither!"

They would laugh.

"Was there a village then?"

"Oh sure, that hasn't changed anyway – same old place, exactly the same as the day I could sit up and see."

"Then what's changed?"

"Oh well! Everything is changed, everythin'!"

"Like what?

"Like, ah, like, ah..." He would shrug and throw his hands up, shaking his head as he retrieved the memories from a time no one else could claim.

"We've changed!" he finally declared.

"How's that?"

"Well..." He would consider, lifting his cap and scratching, tapping his pipe on his knee until finally explaining. "We listen to the women more," quickly adding with a look of sudden trepidation, puckering as if he had just bit down on something sour, "Women now run the place! The world has gone to market in a fish basket, I tell ya! In a fish basket!"

Everyone laughed and patted him on the back. No one mentioned his glass eye – that was a sensitive point. A fishhook had plucked it out, the line cast by Freddy.

Abigale would inevitably respond. "Now Pappy...," gaining his attention as he absorbed the applause, kicking back in his chair, sucking on the stem of his pipe.

"...Pappy? ...Pappy!"

The chair pitched forward.

"My love?"

"Tell us how grateful you are that that is true!"

"Of course, my love; of course!" and he would turn to his adoring crowd to add, "...And I'm very grateful too! Very grateful!" as he kicked back to the explosion of laughter that filled Abigale's porch.

Later, Abigale took Pappy aside.

"That was silly."

"I'm sorry, my love; I couldn't help it."

"You're not even a bit like that."

"Well, sometimes I'd like to be. I sometimes find myself... well... a bit boring, that's all."

Abigale considered. "Maybe in another lifetime, then," she said and smiled.

"Sure. ...Do you think you could arrange it?"

"Absolutely, why not?"

They both laughed knowing that some things are, indeed, impossible.

"That's a just a little anecdote I thought you might appreciate," Alessandra said on finishing. "It just might give you a sense of what they were really like. I miss them horribly."

FRANCIS

"Did Francesco arrive in this world via the river?" Patrick asked trying not to sound facetious.

"No, just me – and my mother, too, of course, and her mother before her, and so on, and so forth."

"I see."

"It just took a while in my case; that is why Abigale reacted so strongly when I finally did arrive. She imagined she had done something wrong when nothing could be further from the truth.... But you knew I would say that, didn't you?"

"How did you meet Francesco? Originally, I mean: the first time."

"I think I have told you all about that many times – it barely needs repeating. We honestly do not have time for it. It is the snowball in July story."

"Oh, right. I love that one."

"I thought you were too old for stories?"

"I recall Bekele and me laughing." Patrick smiled, remembering. "Snowballs – who would have thought such things were possible!"

"Alessandra smiled back. She cleared her throat, and then frowned, and then brightened and began. "Once, Francis, often alone among the children – that's wrong; I don't know why I mindlessly repeat it; Francis was *never* alone; he was very popular with us all; he was such a card, not unlike Pappy – shattered a shop window with a snowball in July. He had saved the perfectly formed projectile all year in Abigale's icebox, intending to ambush young Alessandra, of all the young girls he could choose – and if he hadn't where would we be today, eh? – on the hottest day of the year." The image of poor Alessandra opening the front door of her home, stepping out into sunshine, lifting her face to it, turning with her hand on the door to ensure it wouldn't slam, would remain with Francis forever, often summoned when he thought of her. "Only Francis could have written such bumf, only he," Alessandra exclaimed. "I have no idea why he said it all the time. It is silly. By the way, not so poor, actually; I could have dunked the overconfident, somewhat clownish, Francis in the river any time I felt like it just for the fun of it. But back to the story such as it is.... But what Francis did not realize on that careless day was that his snowball would never be allowed to strike the likes of Alessandra; she might have been hurt, and no one wanted to hurt Alessandra Elizabetta Marsh in any way; not her, of all people. Good plan! Good plan, I say! It was therefore inevitable that the perfectly shaped sphere, once in perfect flight, would inexplicably alter course and shatter Vaughan's plate glass display window two doors down. It took me a while to figure out how to do that: three tries in fact," Alessandra stated.

"Anyway, that is the truncated version; we do not have time for the full version right now, Patrick. Later, perhaps, or we will otherwise never finish. Look, it is already three in the morning!"

"This was your idea! But one minor change: I thought it was your bedroom window that was broken, not the plate glass window two doors down."

"Ah! Details, details; it changes nothing, really! Let me continue with the story.... Ruthie named your father Francis – John Francis Wilson, meaning for everyone to call him John but Francis stuck. Ruthie Anne Wilson was your grandmother and my mother's best friend. Both gone up to the *Nappin' Place* long ago. Your grandfather on your father's side was, of course, Fred – long gone; a week or so before Ruthie. By the way, do you know why men often die before their wives? ...Because they want to! Ha! Anyway, his full name was Fredrick Thomas McHarg – Pappy called him Freddy, but most just called him Fred. Best of friends, best of friends, always; both dead; both gone, long ago."

Alessandra continued. "And as far as changing his name goes, from Francis to Francesco, your father only called himself Francesco after he followed me to what used to be called Zimbabwe; he said to anyone from here who might ask, and no one really did since they knew what he was like, that he thought it more glamorous. But the truth is, he thought changing his name to Francesco Alfonso Tosselli – you remember what your father was like with names – might help him get a position with the Italians. The truth is he changed his name for the simple reason he needed a job, and the Italian Consulate had one ready and waiting if only he was Italian and could speak Amharic or Oromo. As you well know, your father was brilliant with language, and, as such, he was a shoe in; his name would not have mattered, as it turned out. We laughed about it for years, us and the Ambassadors and the consular officials that came and went over the years, and always over a bottle or two or three of Chianti, which we always supplied. Of course, they ultimately gave him an Italian passport no questions asked – they, meaning the Italians, did that sort of thing in those days.

"And, yes, it is true, you inherited that gift of language from your father; all of us here have one or more gifts that make us rather special, gifts that we tend to inherit. God knows what you inherited from me, Patrick; your sense of humour, maybe?" Alessandra laughed. Catching Patrick's reaction, she added more solemnly, "...Or maybe not?"

"Or maybe not."

Alessandra laughed, throwing her head back, slapping her knee.

HOW

"So, I suppose you want to know how your mother could somehow find a way to cure Emily while you and yours could not. You should know that there is nothing supernatural about it, or fantastical or magical; it is just that my science is better than yours. You see, the truth is we all came from Beetlejuice – we had to leave; our sun was acting weird: losing mass, spinning up; it is going to blow up one day – no time soon but less than a million years from now which is soon enough, and far too soon for us. Anyway, we landed here, or close to here, somewhere around here anyway, about a thousand years ago and called it home and we haven't looked back since." Alessandra sat back. "You should see the look on your face," she added, carefully controlling her smile. "It is nothing for you to feel ashamed about; it is not your fault. You will catch up eventually." Watching Patrick's shifting expression, she added, "Okay, so if you really want to know, we find all the little parts that don't belong and remove them one by one – it is not done overnight; it does take a while. I think you call it mitochondrial DNA which is expressed in the twenty-five thousand or so human genes. The body is a machine; we fixed the machine; we are not miracle workers."

By then it was well past three and dawn seemed very far away.

Patrick sat back as Alessandra had. "Fine, let's move on," he said.

BORN IN THE VILLAGE

"Sorry, Patrick, but I forgot to tell you last night – Good morning, by the way; breakfast is on its way. How did you sleep?"

"I recall nothing of the two hours and thirty-six minutes that have elapsed since we broke off last evening, close to dawn, if I recall. Please don't tell me you left something out."

"I did, and it is important."

Patrick sat at the kitchen table, landing hard and all at once.

"Coffee will be ready in five, eggs in six, toast in seven; but it is like this, Patrick, and it is why this is important. There is no way you could know but you were born right here in the village, and in this house too." Alessandra indicated upstairs. "In the room you are in now, in fact."

That surprised him. He almost said something.

"Not delivered by the river, or a stork, or some such thing?" he did say.

"No, no, nothing like that! Your birth was quite normal. The entire village was packed into our home: endless pots of tea, untold trays of blueberry muffins; it was quite the day. Your father was a wreck, completely jet-lagged from our quick trip from home in Kenya, where we lived at the time. I was not worried at all; I knew you would be just perfect, and you were and so remain!" She caught his eye and smiled. "It was May 11th – that hasn't changed, has it? And on one of the most beautiful springs ever! I will never forget it!"

The toast popped. Alessandra hustled to butter it. "I thought seven minutes; it's early but it is quite toasted. Anyway, we went back to Kenya two weeks later after spending less than three weeks here. Time does not mean much here – staying short or long does not matter. Abigale wanted to leave you here with her, but I wouldn't have it. I wanted you to grow up in the world as it is, and so you did, didn't you? I don't know; I still think sometimes I should apologize. But it has been good for you in the long run, I think, hasn't it?" Alessandra turned to face him. "Right?"

"And the lorry? The number forty-two?" Patrick asked, eyeing the toast as Alessandra poured his coffee.

"A splash of cream it is.... Oh yes, that was silly, wasn't it? That was your father all over. I really do miss him – not that he has gone anywhere."

"Why didn't you simply tell us the truth?"

"Well, because this place is quite the secret, you know. I felt quite obliged not to. But I did give out hints here and there I am sure you can see now. I did try in my own way."

Patrick prompted. "The eggs."

"Oh!" Alessandra removed them from the heat, and immediately ran cold water over them. "Seven-minute eggs; they will be a little hard. I prefer them a bit yolky, and I know you do; sorry about that."

"It is not a problem – and the coffee is excellent, by the

way. An Ethiopian blend?"

"It is."

"How do you do it, Alessandra? More to the point, *why* do you do it?"

Alessandra turned and faced him. "Ah, yes, there is that, isn't there? It is simple, Patrick; this is your home and I want you to stay, and I thought a good breakfast would help."

She sat at the table across from him and dropped her chin into the palm of her hand.

Patrick reached out and helped himself to another piece of toast. "You are quite right."

ANOTHER THOUSAND YEARS

None of this happened. It is all make-believe.

"I have lived here all my life and I understand so little," Pappy sighed, taking in a deep breath and letting it out slowly. They sat on the edge of the jetty, the boathouse to their backs. "It's a real mystery!" He placed his pipe back into his mouth and pulled on the cold stem. "Argh! That's out!"

Patrick was just clearing twenty-one years old, more than old enough to tease his grandfather. "Maybe you're not all that smart, Pappy – maybe that is your problem. Did you ever think of that?" It was the year before he left for London to study medicine. Four years later Pappy would be dead, his skull hitting the river ice at high speed barrel jumping with the Stapleton kid.

"I'm damn near old enough to figure it out if it was something anyone is meant to figure out," Pappy quickly threw back, tapping the burnt tobacco out his pipe, placing the remnants into his pocket.

"Exactly how old are you? I know it is not polite to ask but how old are you? A thousand years? Two thousand?"

"I lost count long ago."

"And Alessandra?"

"Older."

Patrick laughed, playing along. "How can that be, she's your daughter! I'm twenty-one."

Pappy slowly nodded. "Well, that's something. It's a good start." He reached across and turned Patrick's head from side to side. "Handsome bugger...."

"I take after Alessandra."

Pappy laughed. "You can't go too far wrong there, I guess!" He sat back and kicked his feet, swinging them back and forth as if swimming on his back. "Tonight, I feel like a kid...."

Patrick laughed again.

"Your grandmother is pretty smart; now she's my wife so I gotta say that. But Alessandra now.... Now she's something else! She's smarter than both of us put together, and that's saying something given how smart I am and how smart you're goin' to be one day."

Patrick checked his reply keeping his smile.

"Do you know what Alessandra calls the world?" Pappy continued. "Has she told you yet, Patrick, my boy?" Pappy stared out over the river as the sun set the final bit and the sky turned a deep orange, silver and gold. "The world is like a quilt," he said, paraphrasing Alessandra, "a patchwork quilt, she once told me, full of color and complex patterns that connect and fold back on themselves in beautiful ways – like a kaleidoscope, the patterns repeating but never quite the same. I can see that.... I can see that. I don't understand it, but I see it." He glanced at Patrick. "She says she can see further than the stars, and that is her gift, at least one of them." He sat back. "Now that's a funny thing to say, don't you think? What's beyond the stars? Who the hell knows?"

"Beyond the stars are more stars," Patrick remembered Alessandra saying. He said as much.

Pappy placed his arm around Patrick and drew him close. "A thousand years; what does it do for a fool like me but want another thousand?"

SPRING

May inevitably arrived and it was spring. The snow melted, the river cleared, Francis was free, and the world was reborn. Literally overnight, the snow disappeared, cascading in mad torrents to the tumbling river. A detonation of life: exploding grass, sprouting crocus, and budding leaves – dancing daffodils, cavorting tulips, wild seas of emerald and gold. *The lilac... Ah, the lilac...!* Its perfume mixed with the scent of the vibrant earth and the showers of apple blossoms falling into everyone's garden. A promise made and then fulfilled over, and over again with only slight variation: sprouting grass, pregnant crocuses, and dancing leaves – budding daffodils, cavorting tulips, wild seas of emerald and gold... the scent of lilac! Wild seas of emerald and gold....

"It's to be a good year!" Alessandra announced, and everyone smiled and nodded, casting their arms upward and outward in thankfulness. Never getting enough, missing too much the first time through, the villagers often stepped back onto their porches to pretend that spring was beginning all over again, brushing back their tears as Alessandra promised, yet again, what a good year it would be.

With summer almost upon them, and every villager turned out scrubbed and dressed in their best clothes, men and women, young and old, retrieved Francis from the boathouse determined to plant him in the ground along with the crop. It was a sign of their great respect. Francis had lived amongst them; he had laughed with them, fought with them, cried with them... drank with them...

and they intended to give him a farewell the likes of which had not been seen in the village for countless years – at least not since the last funeral. What they intended this time, however, was unique in its sheer audacity, outrageous in its design, never before attempted, never even dreamed of – but then the times, they were a changin'. There was a new voice in the village, a new vision, a burst of life and energy that meant a bright future for all.

"Emily, love; come here, dear."

Emily accepted Alessandra's hand.

Alessandra kissed her cheek, and then the other. "There now."

The young blonde-haired, green-eyed, red-mittened girl from the ice joined them, and all three held hands.

"The young girl aforementioned is Abigale, by the way – Abigale Alice Smith. Smart. Happy. Pretty – pretty and pretty awesome, that is! Hold onto your socks! She is somethin'! Ha!"

The village crammed into Alessandra's home with the remainder overflowing into the garden beneath the blossoming apple trees surrounded by hyacinth and peony in full bloom. The villagers mingled and chatted, gaily sipping tea, nibbling on wafer biscuits lighter than air and still warm from the oven. A few spirited out flasks hidden in the inner pockets of seldom worn suits or concealed within the complex depths of shiny purses. Some could be seen tipping the contents into the dark tea while glancing left and right, smiling to one another as they did so, and all this while a warm breeze drifted down from the ice-free hills carrying with it the fragrance of freshly turned earth, mown grass, lilac, crab apple, honeysuckle, wild rose in bloom, and pear.

Patrick chatted with new-found friends as beside him, as new and fresh as the spring, Emily floated, seemingly suspended in midair: shining, sparkling, radiating, her arm wound comfortably through Patrick's as apple blossoms drifted downward, some landing on Patrick's shoulders and in his tea, others catching onto thin wisps of Emily's hair, holding for a moment before dropping in a final spiral onto her bare shoulders.

A clutch of villagers mingled on the edge of the garden overlooking the fields, while still others gazed up into the blossoming trees just for the pleasure of it. Some were bent to caress the soft petals and smell the richly fragrant scents of the tumultuous flowers. Those with families sat with their children, holding their hands while sharing their biscuits and tea. They talked and talked, some emphasizing what they meant with expansive gestures, while others sat with their hands carefully folded in their laps and only their chins wagging and their eyes shining. But all carried the conversation, as well as the afternoon, along.

"Who's taking poor ol' Francis up the hill?"

"We all are – what did you think?"

"Tell me we're not takin' him up in that cracking' boat?"

"Of course we are takin' him up in that cracking' boat – what did ya think!"

"McHarg better not be in it! He ain't no feather!"

"Do fish pee in the river? Bears poop in the woods? Of course McHarg is in the crackin' boat – what did ya think!"

And then they'd laugh together.

The villagers made their rounds: first Alessandra, men

and women taking up both her hands, kissing her cheek. The women saying, "Very, very sorry, darling! Very, very sorry! Francis was so good for you, wasn't he? We miss him so and I know you do too!" They would step away but then immediately return, pushing past their husbands to embrace Alessandra in yet another giant hug, kissing her cheeks yet again and then wiping at their eyes before finally moving on, the men sheepishly following, grumbling a little – but never preceding, always falling in behind – and all the while Alessandra in full tears, sobbing and wiping at her nose with a tissue extracted from a pocket when she was not holding someone's hands.

And next, Patrick, the women sighing – he was very handsome, after all – "Patrick, dear, this is so sad! We loved your father so! We will miss him terribly! I know you do!" They kissed him, once on the lips, sometimes twice on his lips, always one more kiss planted on his cheek while their men rolled their eyes, and when it was their turn shook Patrick's hand, slapping him on the shoulder as they trundled past. "Talk later; not now... Gotta go; catch you up. Hey!"

Next in line, Emily, the women kissing her, keeping their rouged cheeks pressed up against her cheek for a long moment saying, "We're so glad you are here!" Then stepping back, generosity spilling from their voices, saying, "You are so gorgeous, dear!" with their tears now in a full cascade, often reaching back and grasping her hand and kissing her yet again saying, "So pretty!" while their men shifted their weight nervously managing only to stutter when it was finally their turn, "My sympathies...," before stumbling on red of face.

The routine became so perfectly predictable that Emily

made a point of mentioning it to Patrick, nudging him in the ribs.

"This is nuts."

"Yes, it is."

"Glad you're back?"

"I have to say yes."

"Not going anywhere?"

"Not now."

"What do you mean, 'not now'?"

"Not now."

Triggered by Alessandra's abundant tears, followed by Emily's, followed by Patrick's, and then young Abigale's, the villagers inevitably followed suit, the women crying with lifted faces and cascading tears, the children following their mother's example, and the men sheepishly wiping away their tears with the sleeves of their shirts.

"Poor Francis – he's dead, you know?"

"Is that why we're here?"

"Oh, do be quiet, Jim! You're just making fun!"

"He's been dead a while."

"Well, he's still dead, you fool!"

Evening settled, hushed, wet earth, spring in the warm air, the stars dancing in a still sky, riotous, insane in their beauty: jumping singularities against the dark, announcing and confirming that eternity was real and all about them. Emily and Patrick had managed to escape to a far corner of the garden waist deep in hyacinths and apple blossoms. Life settled everywhere. Time nearly stopped. Both so tired they could barely stand. Emily leaned back, and a streak of light tore a silent arc across the sky. It originated out of the night illuminating for only a fraction of a second the garden and the stillness of the river before disappearing in an instant over the mountains.

"Alessandra is sitting in her cane-backed chair beneath the trellis," Emily said quietly. "Can you see her?"

Patrick turned his head to look. It was dark, with only the fireflies and shifting shadows dancing across the garden. "No, I don't think so...."

"She is sitting with her hands on her lap, looking right at us, smiling. She can see in the dark, I think."

"Can you?"

"No, not yet."

Patrick leaned in to take in the fragrance of Emily's hair as the stars shifted then jumped above them.

"How long did you say we have?" he asked.

"Hundreds and hundreds of years," she replied. "That's a long time, hundreds and hundreds of years. It is not forever but it is the best we can do."

"That's okay. I'll take it."

THE NAPPIN' PLACE

The next day was like the first day, the very first day, the day of creation, a brand-new day. The villagers lifted Francis, complete with the boat, his fishing rod and half-empty bottle of beer, onto the shoulders of the strongest men and women who were prepared to carry him up the hill to a secret, unmarked, place, the *Nappin' Place*. It was a burial ground where no stone marked a grave. No paths, no signs of man or animal, just a flowing meadow of green and gold leading up from the village. Bounded by the river, snow-capped mountains, a dark forest, and a regiment of giant oak standing as ordered sentinels, thick and tall, broad and reaching, with sunlight filling the green spaces between. No one knew who had planted the oaks, but they were as old as the village, and older than Francis by at least twenty thousand years – or so Pappy had once said when he was twelve and there were those who still remembered.

Robert McHarg shouted from the door of the boathouse as the men shuffled about trying to find the best way to hoist the boat onto their shoulders. Smiling and respectful, they stood aside as Robert, often referred to as Bob, slightly tipsy from already too much of *Jack Rafter's Finest IPA*, stretched a leg over the gunwale. "Easy there! Easy there!" he squawked as he pitched sideways into the boat, landing with a thud. He sat upright holding his middle. "I spilled my beer," he sheepishly explained. Someone handed him a fresh one.

Bob took a long draught then turned to his old friend and saluted. "Time to go!" he cried out, and as the procession turned to head up the steep slope toward the

Nappin' Place, more than a hundred pairs of hands lifted the boat up and over their heads.

Alessandra looked about, shading her eyes against the bright sun. "We need the three of us...." She stretched, standing on her toes to peer out over the sea of heads. She found her son cracking yet another beer and handing it up over the bearers to Bob who, with a foot raised to prop up Francis, was at the same time handing back a clutch of empties.

"Another for the dead guy!"

The procession moved: one step, two, slowly and precariously forward. Francis' back was to the river, his fishing rod apparently forgotten, and his beer mysteriously tossed aside as Bob pointed out the way, remarking as they progressed on the special green of the meadow and the unbroken blue of the sky. The two friends were held by the upraised hands of the village. They floated in the air, held steady within a perfect calm, held suspended upon the undisturbed surface of a river of hands. Up they went, past the home Francis had lived in until he married Alessandra, past the school and church, past the home where Alessandra lived and where Patrick entered the world, through the stand of oak, and finally to the rolling unmarked knolls of Francis' resting place.

It was quite impossible to straighten out Francis' frozen form, so Patrick had his father lifted as he was from the boat and placed on a chair a volunteer had rushed down the hill to fetch. He tied Francis to it, whispering into his frozen ear, "Excuse me, Francesco; sorry about this. The rope will keep you in the chair. You won't fall out. Don't move, okay? Just stay where you are until.... Until you're on the bottom. Then you can do what you want, okay?"

Some of the villagers offered to help. "Jeeze, Paddy, do ya want some help there? You shouldn't need to do this. Patrick, dear, please...."

"No, no, I'm fine, fine."

The men carefully lowered Francis into the earthy darkness, hat straightened, his fishing rod in one hand and a fresh brew carefully placed there by Jack himself in the other. Patrick wept and laughed as the village looked on with barely concealed amusement mixed with tears.

Down Francis went.

"Easy does it!"

Francis was down.

Patrick snapped the release rope and pulled in the ropes that had lowered him.

"That just about does it," someone said.

"Yep," Bob McHarg managed, adding, "Yeah, well... poor old bugger! You'll be most of next spring, I suppose."

The bearers turned the boat downhill and once again hoisted it onto their shoulders and marched, their pace checked to keep their speed constant and orderly. The remaining villagers turned as one and linked themselves together into a single body. They became a living entity with a heart and a soul in perfect order. They retraced their sad steps back to their homes beside the river, sighing as they went, and not letting go as they went. There would be a special dance tonight, everyone would attend; there would be no exceptions.

Young Abigale stepped out of the background, her blond hair spilling across green eyes. She reached for Emily's hand. "Can I dance with you at the party tonight?"

Emily looked down and smiled; a sad smile and a

careful smile that slowly opened when she saw who had asked.

"I don't see why not."

The girl smiled back; she shrugged her shoulders, her smile suddenly exploding to say, "Thank you!"

She turned to go.

Emily called after her. "I like your barrette...."

The girl reached up to touch it as if she had forgotten it was there. "My mom gave it to me."

"It is very cool."

"It's sapphire."

Emily leaned forward to examine the jewel more closely, wisps of the child's hair tickling her nose; she smelled like spring itself.

Emily jumped back. "Ha! I can see myself in it! I can see everyone in it!"

Abigale smiled and ran her fingers over it again.

"Do you want it?"

"No, thank you, it's yours; your mom gave it to you."

Abigale smiled again; she ran backward, turned; then, laughing, skipped ahead to catch up to the others. "I hope you can dance!" she called back over her shoulder.

"See you soon, and yes I can!" Emily lobbed after her.

Emily and Patrick took the long road home, their lover's arms linked. They glided, floating above Earth. Only two remained behind, Alessandra and Bob; together they filled in Francis' grave one last shovel-full at a time.

ALL OF THIS

The sun lingered, white and pure against the folded blue of the sky, etching the snow-capped mountains to the horizon, turning the leaves more green than green, the river more blue than blue, the morning clearer than winter's ice. Emily stood in the river up to her knees, her dress pulled high, her face to the sun, her eyes closed; her hair, longer now, falling to her shoulders. She bent, one hand to hold her dress, the other reaching for the water, just to feel the velvety cool softness of the river, just to connect the sensation from her toes to her fingertips.

Straightening, she called out, "It is an exceptional morning, don't you think?"

Patrick stood concealed behind the rushes, the tall and reaching maples and crowding lilac in full bloom. He was not surprised she knew he was there.

"A most exceptional morning."

Emily turned fully to him and smiled. "I call, you come running... I like that about you."

"Present me with an occasional treat, and I come a runnin'!" He laughed.

"Occasional? I am afraid, you require much more maintenance than that!"

Patrick laughed again, joyous and light; spontaneous and warm, as Emily stepped out of the river to join him. The hem of her dress fell into place as he kissed her. She remained close, her forehead to his.

"This is nice."

"It is nice – but you realize this was the day of the climb," Patrick said, not letting her go, nor she him. "My pack is packed, I have my boots on, the others are waiting," he added.

"Mountains are very good at waiting."

They sat side by side along the bank, leaning back onto their elbows, fingers entwined, feet outstretched, gazing out over the river.

"You are in a mood today," Patrick said.

"I am, very much so. There is something...." She kept her eyes on the rippled surface, searching its length, catching where a wind spilled from the bank, touched the surface, and caught the sun. "All things fold upon one another, do they not?" she mused, not expecting Patrick to answer. "It is a strange and wondrous world we have inherited. I understand so little."

"Now you sound like Alessandra."

Emily smiled. "She does rub off on you. I am very much quoting her." She turned to him. "You are very perceptive, Doctor Marsh; I have often noticed that about you."

Patrick settled an errant strand of her hair back behind her ear. "What's up, why did you call?"

"You should always tell someone if you love them, shouldn't you?" she said. "You might never get another chance. You have to know, then, that I love you." She turned back to the river and opened her arms. "And all of this!"

Patrick slowly nodded. "Okay, this is not the Emily I know. What has got into you?"

She remained focused on the river. "Everything."

"Should I be afraid?"

She smiled, turning back to him. "That depends."

"On what?"

"That is entirely up to you."

"Okay, and you called me because?"

"Because it is time."

"Time?" Patrick asked. He thought and then realized what she meant. "*Oh, time...!*" He sat up straight.

"This is your lucky day as it turns out. I wasn't sure until just a few moments ago – hence the summons."

Patrick nodded. "That's good... good!" He glanced at her and then smiled. "Finally!"

They both laughed as they lay together on the soft moss, sunlight and shadows dancing around them as the river flowed.

TELL IT TO ME AGAIN!

Patrick reached for Emily who lay somewhere beneath the sheets of their great bed. He found her close, her warmth radiating outward as if from the sun, giving her position away. He drew himself near, resting his head on her pillow, her scented hair tickling his nose. Their bodies matched, the shared heat enfolding them as his hands slipped along her body, sensing before feeling the soft and blazing contour of her flesh. He wrapped his arm about her waist and drew their bodies tightly together as he matched the rising and falling of her breast to his slow breathing, remembering how Emily had once said that this was how they would live forever.

"Do you think Alessandra and Francesco were ever like this?" she had once asked, leaning over him, her hair loose about her. They had been in bed since the early evening, their dinner still on the table.

"I'm sure they were."

She settled her chin on his chest. "You should always tell someone you love them, if you do," she said.

"Yes, it's very important."

"Hmmm..."

"...Well?"

"Well, what?"

He lifted her off him, suspending her in the air, and then let her down until her body hovered over his – and they kissed, and made love.

Tell it to me again....

Ha!

Emily awakened in the early morning with the sun just

lifting from the river, turning their curtains and lace to gold. She stretched, turning through his arms onto her back. There was no world outside – no garden with heart-red scarlet sage, no barrows of prim chrysanthemums, no fields of endless green, no misty forests warming in the sun, no river of seamless silver, no sky of boundless gold, no precipitous mountains with their lavender peaks, no village.

"Mornin'..."

"Mornin'..."

Patrick let his hand fall across her sleep-warmed body, under the covers and along the wondrous curve of cheek and neck, brushing across the promise of her breasts, to rest on the slight swell of her tummy.

"When are you going to tell me: a boy or a girl?"

He could feel her smile.

She reached up through the sheets to touch his face, her fingers lingering on his lips before returning to the warmth within.

She asked with sleep still in her voice, her eyes half open, "What time did you get to bed last night?"

"Not too late, but I saw a wonderful thing – the sun chasing a diamond star down toward the horizon. They were like two living things, each lingering before finally letting go and plunging into the darkness of the river. It's a sure sign that winter is almost over."

He moved to get up. "If you really want to know, it was the planet Venus, and the sun just the sun."

"Wait...!" Emily pushed him back, leaving her hand on his chest as if to measure the rate of his heart. "Wait right there."

Patrick settled back, smiling. She read his thoughts

and laughed, drawing out her response. *"Nooooo...!"* Shaking her head, rubbing her nose against his, laughing, repeating, *"Noooooo!"* Catching her breath, smiling, waiting for him, she added, suddenly serious, "There's something I must to tell you." She sat up and leaned over him, drawing the sheets about them to keep in the warmth. The sun, through the lace, caught in her hair, once again changing everything; how could anything be the same after that?

"There are so many things I don't understand, my love; I weep that I cannot," she said.

Patrick had sensed the seriousness in her but that took him by surprise.

"What do you mean?"

"All I know is that the currents run dark and deep – dark and deep and riotous with color."

Patrick pushed himself up onto his elbow as Emily fell back onto her pillow. He looked into her eyes for her meaning as she reached again for his hand, drawing it to her, laying it on her tummy.

"Her name is Elizabetta," she said. "You will call her Lizzy," and the mystery of their world folded, once again, upon itself.

ACKNOWLEDGEMENTS

This work would not be the same except for all those with Atmosphere Press, notably Nick Courtright, Kyle McCord, Cameron Finch, and Kelleen Cullison who made *The Glorious Between* a whole lot better. My grade 12 English teacher, Mrs. A. Kennedy who made all the difference by believing in me as a writer. Ed Mieczaniec of the same era who taught me that good writing is an artform that takes years to master. Ben Ballard for his support as well as giving me a place to write at the old Ballard farm in Maryland. Adrian Hill, Annette Mirantes, Debbie Clancy, and Tim McGee for their friendship and support. Robin Vaughan for her exactitude and reading through early prototypes. Neil Bobroff and Arnold Davenport for their continuing support and encouragement. Hermine Steinberg for organizing a place where I could learn. Selina Appleby for her friendship, wisdom, and guidance, in addition to the odd cup of tea now and then. Judy Odom and Barb Carroll for their encouragement while letting me know what they liked and what they didn't which was very important to know. Jim Wood, aka *Mister Wood!* for his long-time friendship and enthusiasm, and especially his ability to read through some of my rawest prose and still be encouraging. A special thanks to Terry Belleville for his friendship and expert advice and for keeping me focused on what is important in writing and why we write. My late mother and father, Margaret and Clarence, aka *Pappy*, Reid, who I think would be quite pleased with what I'm trying to accomplish. Mary Alice Marsh, who I otherwise refer to as Grandma Beckett, whom I think of often, and who might be the main reason why I strive for perfection. And, finally, my immediate family: Alison, Sarah, Eloise, Isla, Mitch, and, most important of all, my wife Patti for her loving patience and unflagging encouragement.

Doug Reid
Maui, Hawaii. 20 March 2020.

ABOUT ATMOSPHERE PRESS

Atmosphere Press is an independent, full-service publisher for excellent books in all genres and for all audiences. Learn more about what we do at atmospherepress.com.

We encourage you to check out some of Atmosphere's latest releases, which are available at Amazon.com and via order from your local bookstore:

Itsuki, a novel by Zach MacDonald

A Surprising Measure of Subliminal Sadness, short stories by Sue Powers

Saint Lazarus Day, short stories by R. Conrad Speer

My Father's Eyes, a novel by Michael Osborne

The Lower Canyons, a novel by John Manuel

Shiftless, a novel by Anthony C. Murphy

The Escapist, a novel by Karahn Washington

Gerbert's Book, a novel by Bob Mustin

Tree One, a novel by Fred Caron

Connie Undone, a novel by Kristine Brown

A Cage Called Freedom, a novel by Paul P.S. Berg

Shining in Infinity, a novel by Charles McIntyre

Buildings Without Murders, a novel by Dan Gutstein

ABOUT THE COVER

The cover was designed and adapted for both paperback and e-book by Nick Courtright of Atmosphere Press. The central figure is representative of how Emily often feels.

She feels as if she has never existed. She feels as if she is tucked up tight, holding her breath, suspended in time.

The central photograph is titled, "Naked redhead young woman underwater,' by the photographer-artist Pavel Kibenko. The name of the model is unknown.

ABOUT THE AUTHOR

Doug Reid has sailed the seas, jumped out of airplanes, climbed mountains, and when he settled down worked for NASA on some really cool stuff that's still out there in deep space somewhere. He graduated from Johns Hopkins University with a Master of Applied Physics, of all subjects. He has been writing since he could hold a pencil in his hand and apply it to paper.

His interests encompass physics, mathematics, music, art, literature, astronomy, paleontology, anthropology, entomology, geology, even religion—but finds the human mind and heart the most interesting and the most perplexing of all.

He has English roots, some Scottish peat in his blood, and even a twist of the Irish. He can be reached via jdreid1po.com.